Dedication

We dedicate our book to
our many teachers of
English and Literature
who encouraged us to write.

Also, to our family for forbearance as we
labored with researching and writing.

We thank our grandchildren who
have been helpful critics.

Jack and Judith Woods

CHAPTER ONE

As soon as Mr. Robbins said "School dismissed," Jonathan quickly slipped out of his seat. He maneuvered his way to the front of the schoolhouse in the direction of the door. Before he reached it, his farm friend Edward grabbed his shoulder and Jonathan turned to face him.

"Do you have to go right home?" Edward questioned as they skipped down the broad slate steps.

"Why, what do you want to do?" came the reply.

"Let's go down to the canal and see what's there," Edward said.

The two boys were especially interested in the canal at this time of the year. The Erie Canal had just opened up for the season, and all sorts of debris would appear between the banks. There were odd pieces of wood, floating carcasses of deer, groundhogs and other animals that had drowned in the frigid canal water. As they crossed the grassy area bordering the canal, both boys hurried closer to identify a number of small, light brown objects bobbing in the murky water of the canal.

"They're—they're eggs!" shouted the boys.

Edward picked up a long branch from a bush and tried to sweep an egg to within his reach. Although the muddy bank was slippery, he managed to grasp a floating egg without sliding into the canal and brought it up for examination. As he did, the egg exploded in his hand!

The terrible smell of rotten egg filled their noses, and the foul liquid spotted their clothes. Edward gagged, and put his hand over his mouth and nose, looking as if he would throw up. Jonathan ran a few steps away, his nose pinched shut.

"Ohhh!" he groaned. "Wash it off, Edward."

His friend pulled off his foul-smelling shirt, then hesitated.

"The canal's dirtier than the shirt," he choked out.

He threw the shirt away from him, and splashed a little water on his face and arms, all the while spluttering because of the smell. Jonathan soon did the same, his shirt sleeve needing more rinsing than his face and arms. As the shock of the incident began to fade along with the smell, the boys started to smile, then giggle, and soon threw themselves on the ground with howls of laughter.

When they could laugh no more, Edward gasped, "None of our chicken eggs ever blew up like that!"

"No wonder they float—with all that rotten stuff inside," Jonathan said. "I'd like to take one to...," his voice faded away as they both turned toward the sound of hoof and harness of an approaching team on the other side of the canal.

They exchanged mischievous glances, and reached for the branch to sweep in more rotten eggs. By the time the mules and driver were some twenty yards away, they had five eggs between them. They hurried, but remembered to handle the eggs like the fancy glassware in the mercantile store downtown. They sat in the grass looking like innocent schoolboys curious to see the canal boat float by, and carefully lined up the eggs in the soft spring grass. When the mules and driver were directly across from them, they stood up and aimed for the mules' broad sides, and let fly!

One egg fell short, and the splash and putrid odor alerted the driver and spooked the near mule, which sidestepped and moved around as much as the harness allowed. The second and third eggs found their mark, with a resulting pop that could be heard across the canal.

"Hey! You!" hollered the startled young driver —then the next words were choked back by the foul eggs.

Just as well, because the words were as foul as the eggs. Jonathan and Edward were laughing now, and throwing the eggs at the same time. One hit a mule and the last hit the bank. The mule driver struggled with the reins as the lunging and sidestepping were brought under control.

By this time the captain had heard the commotion and was in the bow of the boat, adding his foul language to that of the hoggee. The captain was shaking his big fist and seemed to be looking for something—anything—to throw at them. The boys knew that there was no way for the boat crew to get their hands on them, and they sat down as they grew weak from laughter. The captain angrily stomped back to the stern of the canal boat, where he stared at the two boys.

The boys slowly stopped laughing, scrambled to their feet, and ran away from the canal bank. By the time they got into the open field they were running at top speed. Jonathan began to think of the possible consequences of their actions.

What if they had been recognized? What if that captain did business with Jonathan's father?

When they finally slowed and sprawled in the grass, Jonathan said, "D'ya think we'll get caught?"

Jonathan looked at his friend carefully.

Edward's round face was surrounded by curly dark hair. The early summer sun was already beginning to tan his face and arms. Jonathan thought that Edward looked like a miniature of his father as he brushed his hair from his dark eyes.

Edward squinted from the sunlight as he looked back at Jonathan. He admired Jonathan's lanky height, and could see why people sometimes looked twice at the boy. His hair was the color of dark straw, and had a wave at the front that dipped just over his bright blue eyes. His mouth was quick to smile, and his laugh seemed to tumble out. Instead of a tan, Jonathan's freckles were beginning to show on his face and long slender arms.

Their eyes met, but neither spoke because they had no answer to Jonathan's question. Suddenly serious, the boys started for home, occasionally looking back toward the canal.

By the next morning, it seemed that Jonathan had forgotten about the egg-throwing adventure. He finished his chores earlier than the usual time, and started down Penny Street toward school. Today he was going to go home with Edward after school was out to help on the farm. He could hardly wait!

As soon as Jonathan saw Edward on the dirt road, he hollered and held up a bundle made up of a change of clothes.

"I can stay!" Edward responded by stretching his arms up and shouting.

It wasn't easy for them to concentrate on their studies. Several times during the school day, Mr.

Robbins tapped the ruler on a desk in the front row and chided them for daydreaming.

After what seemed like a long day for the boys, school was dismissed, and they started at a trot for Edward's family farm. Jonathan loved farming, or so he thought. He had helped Edward with chores, and liked the physical activity and the smell of the hay and even the cows. He had not, of course, worked from sunup to sundown for seven days a week. Even this short time doing chores would be an exciting time for the boys to be together as friends.

After changing into chore clothes, Edward and Jonathan received their job to do before milking—cleaning and oiling the team's harness. It was dirty and salty from the sweat and dust of spring plowing. Edward's father thought it would be a good job for them. Jonathan would be enthusiastic about helping and Edward would want to show his friend how well he could work. The job took longer than either boy thought, but Edward's father gave them a big grin and squeezed their shoulders.

"Nice job, boys. Wash that Neatsfoot oil off and see if your sisters have got all the cows in. Time to milk!"

Jonathan couldn't help smiling. He wanted to help with the milking very much, although Edward said that his father probably wouldn't allow it. All but two of the cows were in the barnyard pushing toward the barn door. Edward's sisters were driving the last two down the lane toward the barnyard.

"What's the matter, girls? Won't they do what you tell 'em?" Edward taunted his younger sisters.

The older girl threw a stone at Edward in response, but it wasn't even close. Her anger disappeared when she saw Jonathan.

"Hello, Jonathan," she smiled broadly. "I'm glad you're here."

"Hello, April," he returned. "Glad to help."

The five youngsters shooed the cows inside the barn. Smelling the molasses that was mixed with the ground up feed, they pushed their way to a space in the row of cows and stood in place eating like the others.

The fourteen cows all had names such as Spot, Brownie, and Mary, but Jonathan was only able to identify the obvious Brownie. As the milking progressed the boys carried pails of fresh warm milk to the spring house where Edward's mother strained the milk and poured it into large tinned cans. These cans were picked up by a man who delivered it to people around town.

As each cow was milked, the boys released the cow to spend the night back in the pasture. When the milking was complete, the girls took all the milking utensils to be washed, and Edward's father worked with the boys sweeping and scraping the dairy floor. They shoveled the muck and straw out the side door, and when the pile was big enough, it would be spread from a wagon to fertilize the fields in the fall. The boys made sure the cows were out of the barnyard and into the pasture. Then they placed the gate rails to keep the cows there.

Jonathan smiled again. "I love to do this farm work," he said.

Edward shook his head. "You'd get tired of it if you had to do it all the time," he replied.

Surprised by his friend's response Jonathan said nothing.

They walked to the end of the farm lane near the house and Jonathan said, "Thanks for letting me come over. See you tomorrow in school."

"Ayeh, it was fun working together," Edward smiled. "G'night." Jonathan called over his shoulder. "G'night."

CHAPTER TWO

When Jonathan walked into the schoolroom the following morning, Edward was already in his seat and appeared to be busy at something. He also looked very serious all morning, and avoided Jonathan's eyes. Jonathan wondered if Edward had somehow been caught for egg throwing, and was he going to be next? When they were dismissed for the noon meal Edward did not even wait to talk with Jonathan before running home to eat. Just after recess was over, Edward slid into Jonathan's seat.

"I need to talk with you," he said gravely. "I'll try to get over to your house before milking time, if not maybe you can come over to our place after supper."

Jonathan hissed a whispered, "What's wrong?" but there was no answer as Edward hurried back to his own desk and his studies.

Jonathan wondered what it was all about. Finally the school day was over—Mr. Robbins having said the anxiously-awaited, "School's dismissed!"

He watched Edward race out of the building. Edward was well down the dirt road toward their farm by the time Jonathan got to the front door.

Jonathan started for home in the other direction, not hearing the greetings and happy talk of schoolmates as they walked by him along the street. As he passed the fenced yards along the way, it was obvious that the end of the long central New York winter was finally here. The many long brown stalks of weeds moved in the chill breeze, and bright green leaves were beginning to push up to replace them. Inside some of the yards, gardens which were already planted with early peas now showed tiny plants poking up through the recently frosty soil.

Jonathan noticed the dandelions pushing up through the cracks in the slate walk, and he smelled the wild onions that he stepped on from time to time. Jonathan turned the corner onto Penny Street and walked the dozen steps to the first gate. As he pulled the latch his eyes moved to the building which stood on the far side of the yard. He could hear his father's hammer ringing on the anvil.

As he fastened the gate and turned to go up the walk to the house, he smiled as he saw the neatly laid bricks under his feet. They were his own mother's doing. She worked out the design, and painstakingly laid the bricks in the sand. The walk was about the only sign left of her, other than himself, which remained at the house on Penny Street. The cholera epidemic took her in death in the same month that his father's brother, Uncle Jonas, died. Nearly every family in Rome had felt death caused by the dreaded disease. His father had remarried in less than a year. His step-mother Catherine was only seven years older than Jonathan. She came into their small family with a determined will to make this her home, and to have things the way she wanted them to be. The soft green wallpaper in the front parlor, that his mother had chosen, was now covered over with new. The hand-loomed draperies that his mother had made by hand were gone.

Jonathan supposed that he should feel proud that his father could afford such niceties when they weren't even needed. Instead, he shook his head with a mixture of disgust and bitterness. He saw Catherine in the backyard testing the clothes on the line to see if they were dry. Her bulging silhouette upset him even more. It would not be long before a baby would join their family. Jonathan was sure that the new little one would capture more of his father's heart and time, leaving less for him.

His heart sank as he wondered why their lives had to change. *She has changed everything,* he thought angrily. His father had even called in a carpenter to add six more feet to the end of the house for her. Light yellow paint now covered the comfortable white-washed walls of the kitchen. The red and white curtains and table cloth that had brightened his mother's kitchen were replaced with blue gingham ones made with cloth purchased at the mercantile. A water pump on a cabinet now stood in the corner of the new part of the kitchen. His mother had hauled water into the kitchen in all kinds of weather from the well pump in the back yard.

Every day Jonathan reminded himself of the things which caused him to feel angry and bitter toward his young step-mother. The tidy kitchen itself made him feel uncomfortable. He looked around at all the new things—crockery, plates, and tin ware. As Jonathan walked toward the stairs, he smelled the wonderful smells of baking bread, and of roasting meat. At least she can cook, he thought. Jonathan opened the door to the pantry under the stairs. He helped himself to a piece of Johnnycake and closed the door quickly. He hurried up the stairs to his room to eat, away from the watchful eyes of his step-mother, who by then was heading back to the kitchen from the yard. She called his name as she entered the kitchen.

"Jonathan! Are you upstairs? You'd better not be eating in your room again."

"And why not?" he muttered to himself.

His own mother had allowed him to do this after-school snacking anywhere he chose. Catherine would allow him and his father to eat only at the table. Her over-zealous neat and tidy ways made him bristle!

"I'm up here changing out of my school pants, so I can go out and help Pa!" he shouted down the stairs, now that his mouth was empty.

He quickly changed into his work pants and threw his school pants on the bed.

"Mind you hang up your school pants," came the reminder.

"Oh, all right," he growled, and turned to grasp the pants and hang them on a wooden peg on the wall.

He smoothed the quilt on his bed, and before he

left the room, looked for any stray cornbread crumbs. As he reached the foot of the stairs, Catherine stood facing him. She was only a head taller than Jonathan, and he had gained a couple of inches on her within the short time she had been his step-mother. Her long, light brown hair was braided and neatly pinned up on the top of her head. Her complexion was rosy from the wind, and her hazel eyes sparked as she chided Jonathan.

"I see there's a piece of Johnnycake missing," she accused. "How many times must I tell you that eating is to be done only at the table, and baked goods are only for meals! There's dried apples for chewing on between meals, young man, and you'd better give a listen to me," she quickly went on. "I want you to run down to the mercantile for me. Get two spools of thread, a packet of sewing needles, and a thimble."

"I have to go to the shop," Jonathan returned evenly.

"Your father knows that you'll be doing an errand for me first," she responded.

Realizing there was no sense arguing, Jonathan relented. "Tell me again what I'm to bring back," he said in a defeated tone.

"Well, that's more like it," Catherine smiled back at him. "I need thread, black and white, needles, and Miss Farmer has a thimble put away for me. You can scoot in the back door when you get back, put everything on the table, and be on your way to the shop." She smiled again—warmly and with hope in her eyes for an improving relationship with her stepson. "Have Miss Farmer put it on our bill, Jonathan."

CHAPTER THREE

Jonathan did scoot—right off the back steps before Catherine could think of more errands for him to do. He grumbled to himself all the way to the mercantile. The bell on the door jingled as he opened it. Jonathan went inside, his eyes gradually adjusting to the semi-darkness of the store. He stood and waited on the round braided rug in front of the large glass-topped counter. The dark wainscoted walls would have made the store look dreary, but Miss Farmer's wares brightened the shop. On the wall behind the counter, shelves almost went to the high ceiling. They were filled with gingham, bright satins, velvet, and wool challis cloth. The wide variety of colors transformed the shelves. The light streaming in the store-front windows gave the shelves the look of a kaleidoscope.

Miss Farmer pulled the curtain to the back room where she lived, and peered into the shop.

She was chewing on something as she mumbled, "Oh, it's you, Jonathan." She steadied herself with a cane as she came to stand behind the counter. "Come to pick up something for your step-mother, eh?" Then, as she stared at him she demanded, "Well, what is it?"

Jonathan hesitated for a moment, trying to remember the items on his mental list. "What is it, Boy? Out with it," came the impatient order from Miss Farmer.

"Black thread, white thread," blurted Jonathan. "And needles." He blushed in embarrassment.

She moved to fetch the items. "Is that all today?" she asked over her shoulder. "Anything else?" She asked as she pulled the ledger book from the shelf.

She eyed the edge of the book where the tabs with letters of the alphabet stuck out. She opened it to 'H' for Hamilton. She touched the pencil to her tongue and carefully wrote the items and their prices in the big ledger book.

"No, that's all." Jonathan muttered, forgetting the thimble for his step-mother.

"Thank you Jonathan. Say hello to your folks," she said.

Picking up the items from the counter, he said "Yessum, I will."

He hurried out of the store with relief, jamming the sewing supplies into his pocket. In his hurry to finish this errand and get to the shop to work with his father, Jonathan had run the distance to the store. Now, he walked slowly back down the main street. He passed the tavern again as he headed for home. Jonathan remembered that his father had told him to cross over to the other side of the street to keep clear of the riff-raff and troublemakers who frequented it.

Jonathan thought of his father's words, *Best way to keep out of trouble is to stay clear of taverns all your life and go to church on Sundays.*

Since his mother's death, however, they hadn't attended church at all. When she was alive, she read lessons from Proverbs and quoted many times that the Bible is useful for teaching, correcting, and training. She knew in her heart that the Bible stories were true. She had read the Bible aloud evenings, with father and son as reluctant listeners. Ahijah agreed that the Proverbs had meaningful advice for life, but he did not have the "religious experience" in his own life that his wife had. Jonathan, like most boys, especially liked the story about King David and his good friend Jonathan.

Today, Jonathan chose not to heed his father's advice about the tavern. He didn't see how walking in front of the tavern on a sunny afternoon could hurt anybody. As he was passing in front of the main door, a carriage stopped right next to him.

As he admired the polished harness, a young woman leaned out and called, "Boy." Jonathan looked behind him, expecting someone to run to the carriage. "Boy!" she said a little louder. "I have a message for you to give to a gentleman in the tavern. Here's a penny for you. Boy!" the young woman said, with irritation in her voice. "I mean you!"

"Me, Ma'am?" Jonathan answered weakly.

"Of course I mean you," she snapped. "Take this note inside. It's for a Mr. Barnes. He's a drummer. I'm not sure where he is right now. You'll have to ask for him." After pushing the note into Jonathan's hand, she waved him on with her hand. Jonathan could not believe that he actually had the note in his hand and was walking toward the tavern door.

I must be daft, he thought to himself. *If Father finds out that I didn't cross to the other side of the street, let alone walk right into this place, he's liable to get out his belt for me.*

But even with the warning his conscience was giving him, he pulled open the door and walked into the dimly-lit front hallway of the tavern. At first it seemed that no one was around the place, but a long-haired girl wearing a long apron over her dress entered the hall from what appeared to be the cellar stairs.

"Can I be helping you, Lad?" she offered. By this time Jonathan's anxious heart was thudding in his chest.

"I...I'm looking for a Mr. Barnes. A lady wants him to have this note," he said hesitantly. He held it up to prove its existence.

"A lady, is it?" she sneered. "Gi' it here, and I'll see he gets it—save you the trouble of looking for 'im."

He pulled the note back. "No, that's all right," he returned. "I'll deliver it myself—just tell me where I can find him."

"Well, since Pa has the bar locked up until five o'clock, he's prob'ly upstairs in his room. Mr. Barnes is a drummer, you know. He's got his wares displayed all nice and neat in room four. End of the hall, next to the barber shop. He could be in the third floor ballroom, although my Pa says he better stay out of there." The last was barely heard, as she had started walking through another door at the end of the hallway.

Jonathan didn't have a chance to thank her for the help, and he stood for a moment looking through the door toward the bar. The cream-colored walls had pictures of hunting scenes hung just above each of the four long tables lining the walls. A number of mismatched chairs of various shapes and sizes were around each table. The bar was to the right of the door. It looked like a huge wooden cage to Jonathan. Shelves covered the inside walls, which held tankards and many shapes and sizes of bottles. Jonathan thought that when the bar was open, the window was removed for the transaction of business.

He turned towards the darker hallway, and could now make out the stairs leading upward. He was impressed by the design in the carpet on the stairs, and by the bright brass rods that held it to the shape of the steps. At the top of the stairs Jonathan was forced to turn either right or left in the hallway. He could hear parts of a conversation from the left, so he started in that direction. The first door that Jonathan came to in the hall was obviously set up as a barber shop. The door was propped open with a small crock. The man doing the barbering was facing the side wall, but he saw Jonathan in the mirror as he passed through the shop door.

"Who ya lookin' for, boy, or d'ja wanna shave?" The barber laughed as he spoke. The man in the chair chuckled and stretched up to look at Jonathan over the barber's raised arm. The round-faced barber, who had very little hair himself, had scissors in one hand, and a comb in the other.

"Sir," Jonathan said softly, "I'm looking for Mr. Barnes."

"The drummer? Wal, if he ain't in his room—next door—then he's probably up in the ballroom takin' a snooze."

"Where it's quiet!" added the customer.

Jonathan knocked on Mr. Barnes' partly opened door, but there was no answer. He looked inside the small room. It was crowded with cans and bottles—all with pictures of cows, horses and other farm animals. Jonathan ventured cautiously into the empty room, picked up one of the cans, and read, "Weare's Condition Powder for the Horse."

"Well, that's easy," he said out loud. "Mr. Barnes sells medicine to farmers."

He turned and stood in the door sweeping the hallway with his eyes for a clue—and there it was— a sign at the end of the hall. A large hand painted on the board pointed a finger up the stairs. It said "Ballroom." He opened the door and found a narrow well-lighted stairway to the third floor. Jonathan turned the doorknob and let himself into the large sun-lit room. The room was as big as any he'd seen. Chairs lined two of the walls, and at the far end of the room there was a raised platform Jonathan heard the sound of loud snoring coming from behind a long table that was on the platform.

That must be Mr. Barnes, he thought.

He walked down to the other end of the room and there behind the table, a very large man lay stretched out on his back on six chairs. Each time he snored, his mouth opened and his lips and jowls quivered, much like a horse that was blowing after a run.

Jonathan leaned over a bit and softly said "Mr. Barnes." There was no response. "Mr. Barnes!" Jonathan said, this time a little louder. Still nothing. "Mr. Barnes!" Jonathan shouted. The startled man opened his eyes wide and sat up, knocking over several of the wooden chairs as he did so.

He looked around wildly and spluttered, "Who is it? What...what do you want?"

Jonathan wanted to laugh at the bewildered half-asleep man, but he was able to blurt out, "I have a note for you sir, from a lady in a carriage."

"A lady in a carriage?" bellowed Mr. Barnes. "I know no ladies who drive about in carriages. Take your note, you young ruffian and get out of here—immediately!" said the now annoyed Mr. Barnes.

Jonathan had not expected this kind of reception. He turned at once, covering the distance to the stairs in half the time it had taken him to get there, ran down the hall, then down the next set of stairs and was out the door of the tavern in an instant. The lady in the carriage wasn't there any longer. Jonathan dropped the note as if it was a snake and ran across the street to be as far away from the tavern as quickly as he could.

As he hurried on down the street he caught sight of their neighbor Mrs. Tucker.

Oh no! he thought. *I hope she didn't see me come out of the tavern—she'll tell Pa for sure.*

CHAPTER FOUR

When Jonathan got home, he placed the thread and needles on the table, but before he could hop off the back steps he was called back for the short lecture about his forgetfulness, and how vexing it was to his step-mother. He was glad to be away from her, and on his way to the blacksmith shop. He had been helping his father in the shop almost every day since he started school five years ago.

He truly loved working with his father. Jonathan liked to recall the story about the building of the blacksmith shop—he'd asked to hear it many times while growing up. A stonemason was hired to build the shop. He agreed to have Jonathan's father and his Uncle Jonas to assist him in place of his regular helpers. In this way, the cost of construction would be less. They had started on the wall where the forge and chimney would be placed, and when most of that wall was completed, the stonemason got drunk, was severely beaten in a fight, and disappeared from Rome.

Ahijah and Uncle Jonas finished that wall as best they could, but built the rest of the shop from lumber. Each time Jonathan looked at the stone wall, he was impressed because it was so straight and neatly built. The forge was set near the middle of the wall and the bellows was in the left corner. One of his after-school jobs was to pull the wooden handle that lifted the top of the bellows to draw in the air that would blow on the hot coals and in turn heat up the iron to red hot. The iron had to be red hot in order for it to be shaped.

"Never strike blue iron," his father always cautioned.

The anvil was fastened on a tree trunk which was set deep in the dirt floor of the shop. It was placed so that his father could pick up the hot iron, step back with his left foot, pivot his body to his left, and glide the hot iron onto the face of the anvil. As he rested from pumping the bellows, Jonathan watched his father lean over the anvil, use his right hand to hammer, move the hot iron on the anvil with his left, and watch the hot iron take shape. The cooling iron was placed back into the fire while Jonathan got a quick look from his father. He knew that meant to get busy pumping on the bellows. While the iron was heating up, Ahijah raked the soft coal around the ring of the fire, sprinkling water on the outer circle of coal to 'make coke.' The coke burned hot and clean although the continuing process of making coke created black smoke.

His father picked out a clinker from the fire with the tongs, and flipped it on the damp dirt floor. Jonathan still couldn't tell a clinker from good coal. When he tapped it with the tongs, everything seemed to clink—coal, clinker, coke, just everything. He had so much to learn about being a blacksmith. Much of the time his father was very patient with him, but Jonathan was scolded often for neglecting one task or another. His father reminded him that any young apprentice to the trade must remember the instructions that were given. Jonathan stood motionless for a moment while he felt sorry for himself. Jonathan was called sharply back from his daydream by his father's voice.

He began pumping the bellows slowly and evenly to heat the iron for the last shaping of the new tool his father was forging. His father used light hammer blows to smooth the iron and take away any uneven shapes. After the red heat was gone, he dipped the tip of the iron into water and then watched the rainbow of colors creep back down to the tool's tip. Then he plunged the tool into the barrel of water to make it the right hardness. Jonathan's task was to slightly warm the completed tool and rub tallow on it to make it shiny, and to keep it from rusting. He saw Ahijah's smile, and a big sooty hand patted his shoulder.

"Good work, Jonathan!"

That's what he wanted to hear. He couldn't help the feelings he had as he smiled back. His father checked a slate board for the next job to start, and wrestled a piece of iron from the stock rack.

"Pair of buggy springs, Jonathan. Two pieces sixty inches each. Mark 'em for cutting."

Jonathan reached for the measuring stick and a piece of soapstone to mark the iron. This was when he really felt part of the blacksmith trade–when he was given an important task to do. Soon the tedious task of pumping the bellows led Jonathan's mind to other times. He remembered his father's brother, his Uncle Jonas, working in the shop. Uncle Jonas had been a big man, over six feet tall, and was able to swing the heavy sledge easily. What a team they made, working the hot iron together. Both men knew exactly what to do, and much of the time it was all done without words.

Jonathan's eyes returned to his father's form hunched over the anvil, concentrating on shaping the end of the buggy spring. No wonder his father was sharp with him when Jonathan was daydreaming on the job. His father was used to having a partner who understood the trade, who knew what he was doing, as well as what the other should be doing. When the cholera came and so swiftly took away Uncle Jonas and Jonathan's mother, it was very hard on the small family. His father had not only lost his wife, but his brother and business partner. Jonathan could see that there had been a great loss to both him and his father.

Jonathan's mind now wandered in another direction. What if his step-mother's baby is a boy? Would he grow up in the shop as Jonathan had done? Would this new brother take his father's affection from Jonathan?

His father called to him again, "Time to pick up!"

They both set about picking up tools, placing them either on the bench or in the tong rack around the anvil base. He brushed off the black slag from the anvil face, saw the black now on his hand, and a broad smile crossed his face.

"We love to get our hands dirty," they had often told Jonathan's mother.

They didn't say it to his stepmother, because she wanted no soot and iron dirt in the house. He placed the hammer on the anvil with the handle hanging over it. His father said it made it easier to pick up when it was left in that position. Jonathan picked up pieces of iron that he found on the floor, cautiously checking with the back of his hand to be sure they would not burn him. He sorted out scrap from usable iron. The iron would be used by a farmer who lived out in the country. He came by every so often to trade bacon for iron scraps that could be made into nails.

Nails were scarce and somewhat expensive for ordinary folk, so the farmer and his son would heat up the scrap, hammer it out into thin rods, cut them to length, and hammer points onto the nails. This was done with a small forge fire and a special tool called a nail header that his father had made.

After supper, Jonathan asked to visit his friend Edward.

His father answered "Yes, but be home before dark—you know you'll be busy in the shop all day tomorrow."

It took over a quarter of an hour to walk to Edward's family farm. They had just come in from the barn, and dinner was being placed on the large kitchen table.

"Chicken and dumplin's!" Jonathan exclaimed before he realized he said it. "But I can't eat another bite," he quickly added.

He knew that Edward's family of four boys and four girls would need everything in the pot to fill their hungry bellies. He wondered how they could afford such a large family. His father said that on a farm a big family was needed to do all the work. In the midst of all this thinking, Edward's mother made a place next to Edward and his sister April, and he managed to eat a couple of bites of dumpling and thick yellow chicken gravy that April plopped on a plate for him.

Edward had told Jonathan that April is the sister who thinks Jonathan is 'handsome and wonderful', but Jonathan didn't encourage her. She looked too pale and skinny for him.

After the family left the table, Jonathan helped Edward check on the cows in the near pasture. They were content in the lush green spring grass. The chores done, Jonathan waited for Edward to tell him the mystery of Edward's quiet day at school. It came out like a shock.

"We're movin' to the Genesee country," he blurted out. "My father has already sold the farm, and the cows. He even sold the team. We're movin'," he choked on the last word.

Jonathan's shocked eyes smarted and they turned away in silence.

His mind raced as he thought, *What will I do without Edward to talk with, to share, to complain about his step-mother, to...?*

They walked nearly to the back door before either spoke, "I can't believe it. My best friend ever—movin'," Jonathan said through clenched teeth, as he kicked a stone angrily.

Edward took a deep breath and offered, "Paw said that onc't we're settled we could write and see if you could come to visit for awhile."

"How'm I goin' to get there?" Jonathan spit back at Edward.

Edward looked down and slowly shrugged his shoulders in dejection.

"I gotta go, it's near sunset," Jonathan turned and walked briskly toward home.

Edward called from the shadows, "G'night."

Jonathan's eyes smarted, then watered. Soon his grief overwhelmed him, and he sobbed out loud over this new loss in his life.

CHAPTER FIVE

Jonathan spent a bleak Sunday feeling sorry for himself. He was scolded by both his father and step-mother for his sullen attitude. He then spent a miserable Monday in school with Mr. Robbins giving him harsh words for poorly done recitations. Edward was not in school, so when Jonathan left school at the end of the day, his shoulders drooped heavily as he entered the back door of the house on Penny Street. He hung up his school pants, changed into his work clothes, and walked out to the blacksmith shop without even thinking about looking in the pantry for a snack.

His father looked up from his work as Jonathan entered the shop, set his work aside, and went to the bench that served as a desk.

"I've had a letter from your Uncle James. Your Aunt Maude took sick and died last month."

He paused as he dwelt on the sorrow of his own wife, and now her brother's wife dead from the influenza epidemic.

"Your Uncle James says he needs a change—something different to do with his life. He's rented out his farm and bought a canal boat." His father smiled, shook his head, and commented, "That's a change all right!" He paused and stared soberly at Jonathan. "He wants you to help him on the canal boat for the season. I think it would be a good thing for you to do."

At first the words didn't sink in, didn't mean much to Jonathan, but as he stood there, facing the older man, he realized that his father meant for him to leave his home and go to live with someone he hardly knew. Jonathan's mind raced with thoughts of how his step-mother was somehow involved in this, and how this was her way of getting rid of him. He surely couldn't say this out loud to his father, so he only nodded his head.

Jonathan looked at the forge, and said, "Fire's down. Shall I start pumping?"

"Yes." came the short reply.

The sparks flew as Jonathan vigorously pumped the bellows. He eased off quickly because he expected sharp words from his father. As he glanced over at his father, he noticed that he was staring at the cold iron that he was holding with the tongs.

Slowly, his father said, "We'll go to see about a ticket on a line boat to Weed's Basin."

They worked on in silence until it was time for supper.

Jonathan had to wait until the lunch recess to tell Edward about how he was being sent off to his Uncle's to work on a canal boat.

"Well, maybe your Uncle will come west on the canal and we could visit," he said with a hopeful smile.

With that thought, Jonathan's heart lifted, and he said, "Yes, maybe so. Maybe you could come with us for a ride on the canal boat!"

The school bell rang, ending their recess and their hopeful thinking. The boys spent the afternoon doing better with their studies because they were so encouraged by their noontime conversation. Excitedly, they finished each assignment so they could spend time day-dreaming about the changes taking place in their lives. After school, Jonathan and Edward stood out on the slate sidewalk to talk before starting for home. As Edward turned to leave, Jonathan's father appeared.

The surprise of seeing his father at school in the middle of the afternoon showed on Jonathan's face. He gave a final wave to Edward and trotted up the road to meet his father.

"Thought we could go down to buy your ticket before the office closes," his father said.

Jonathan stopped smiling, but nodded his head in agreement.

Seeing the sadness in his son's face he said, "This is not easy for me to do, Jonathan, but as I said I think it will be for the best."

They walked the short distance to the canal office in silence. Even at a half cent a mile, it seemed like a large sum of money to spend. The boat captain had done some business with Jonathan's father before, but there was no dickering for a better price for the fare. Jonathan stood behind his father until he saw that this man didn't look like the captain who was so mad for the eggs thrown at his team.

As Jonathan looked at the newly–purchased ticket, his father said, "We'll have to get you down here at first light on Wednesday."

Jonathan was taken by surprise again. This meant that he would be leaving in only two days! It somehow seemed like a sentence from a judge in court. It was frightening to think about getting aboard a boat full of strangers. His father did his best to encourage Jonathan. He waved a hand toward several canal boats at the dock area.

"I've done business with many of the people. They're good family men who are honest in their dealings and won't let harm come to their passengers. It'll be a safe trip for you."

In the days before Jonathan left, it was hard for both father and son to talk to one another. Since his step-mother came into his life, there was a small but noticeable distance between them. Jonathan wanted to believe that something good would come from this venture, but he wondered how long his father expected him to stay with his Uncle James.

"It's only for the summer, then?" he questioned, as they crossed the yard from the shop.

"Yes, just so Uncle James can get started in the business. You'll miss the end of the school year, but you aren't unhappy about that, are you?"

"No sir!" Jonathan quickly returned. "Not with Edward leaving next week. Say, I'll be leaving before Edward." He stopped suddenly and looked at his father. "I do want to finish the eighth grade, Pa," he said thoughtfully. "How'm I gonna do that if I leave school early in the spring and start school late in the fall?"

"We'll talk to Mr. Robbins about that tomorrow when we tell him that you'll be leaving before the end of the school year," his father said.

Long before first light, Jonathan was dressed in his best shirt, and a coat that his step-mother took special care to brush clean and iron smooth. Most of his other belongings were packed into a black cardboard suitcase that had two leather straps holding it together. Actually, it had one strap and one cord, because one strap had long since disappeared in the loft above the blacksmith shop.

"I can't understand it," his father fussed. "It was all together when I put it up there."

His father said that often–Jonathan thought maybe his father just forgot where things were, and was just making excuses. No matter now, though, if the suitcase stays together, he wouldn't care about the strap. Jonathan, his father, and his step-mother all walked down to the canal landing where he would start on his trip. Jonathan walked along quietly, but his father and Catherine were talking happily and trying to show Jonathan that there was nothing to fear. They told him many times that everything was going to be all right.

"Oh, I'll feel safe enough," he said, "but it's just...." His voice trailed off, not knowing how to say he would miss his father, and that he loved him, especially in front of Catherine.

"Your Uncle James will treat you just fine, you'll see," she said.

"You may meet someone on the boat you can talk to," his father added.

They hugged, and said their good-byes. Then Jonathan and his father stepped aboard *The Pride of Manlius*. The boat had bright yellow paint on every piece of wood that passed for trim. It was everywhere.

"Musta got a good price on yellow paint," his father chuckled.

Jonathan forced a smile. There was some movement through the window toward the bow, and he could see that a pair of mules was being hitched up to the long thick rope that would pull the boat west.

"Well, best be getting off," his father said as he stuck out his hand.

Jonathan grabbed it and they shook hands.

"Good-bye, Father," Jonathan said.

"Good-bye, Son."

Jonathan's father walked over the gangplank without looking back, and soon the boat was in motion. The boy listened to the water trickling past the wooden hull of the boat. He could not hear the sound of the mules' feet hitting the hardened path because they were so far ahead of the boat. The only other boat noise he heard was the sound of the tow rope sweeping across the weeds between the towpath and the canal boat. The noisy chatter of the other passengers called his attention to them— these strangers. He looked out of the window toward his father, who by this time was a small figure that Jonathan saw through tear-blurred eyes. He could not see that his father's eyes were full, too.

CHAPTER SIX

The *Pride of Manlius* moved at a steady pace for hours. It stopped infrequently to let passengers come aboard or to hop off. This portion of the canal was flat and was not interrupted by locking up or down. The first of the three locks the boat encountered before reaching Syracuse broke up the monotony of the trip for many of the passengers. Most had never traveled by canal boat, so they crowded the deck to watch the locking procedure. Jonathan watched through the window. He was impressed by the size of the large wooden doors which fit so carefully into the stone walls of the lock. Some of the stones were as large as a cook stove. The wall reminded him of the wall of his father's blacksmith shop.

Jonathan went on deck after the crowd thinned out and the excitement of locking was over. As they traveled, the black flies and mosquitoes bothered everyone. The men swapped ideas for remedies to keep the bugs away, but no one offered any samples. Jonathan kept slapping and swatting the pests away with his hat. Although the sun had been shining most of the morning, clouds were coming together on the western horizon around noontime. Catherine had fixed and wrapped a parcel of food for him which he planned to eat for his dinner and supper.

The smell of food cooking in the boat's galley made Jonathan wish that he had money to spend for his dinner. His father warned him not to spend money foolishly though, in case he had to pay for lodging once he got to Weed's Basin. There was the possibility that the letter had not reached Uncle James in time for him to meet Jonathan at the dock. When the cook rang the dinner bell, Jonathan went down to the lower cabin to get his parcel. He hurried back to the deck and untied the cord that held it together. Catherine had fixed plenty of food for him. He decided to eat the chicken first and then the slab of pie. He really wanted to eat the second slab of pie because it was so good, but he wrapped the remainder of the food carefully and re-tied the cord.

He stayed on deck until the rain from the dark clouds started to stain the towpath up ahead. He was just settling into his seat on the bench when he heard the rain beating on the deck above his head. The scenery that passed slowly by his window now stopped, and judging from the noise on deck and stairway, more passengers were coming on board. Jonathan's head turned at the sound of people speaking a language he had never heard before. There were a lot of d's and g's and z's mixed in with the words. The man and woman stopped talking and stared back at Jonathan. A grin spread over the man's broad, dark face.

"*Guten Tag,*" the man said.

Jonathan smiled and tipped his cap, but he didn't have any idea what the man said.

A red-faced man sitting a few seats from Jonathan offered, "I heard em talk like that down the Hudson River–it's Dutch."

"Yah, Deutch," the man said as he smiled again.

He pointed at his wife, then himself, and pointed with a great wave toward the west.

"He English not good," his wife spoke. "Ve from Deutchland–Germany–und ve go vest to farm. Railroad give land–ve buy train ticket."

Jonathan smiled, "Farming is good. I like cows." He spoke slowly as if to help them understand.

The red-faced man said, "These boats are full of foreigners goin' west—all the way to Ohio and past the big lakes. I mean a steady stream of em!" He motioned with a wave of his arm. "Most don't talk much English, but they look like hard-working folk. Look at them hands.

Jonathan snuck a quick look at the Deutchman's hands. They were big and thick-fingered. The man's wrists were so big they barely fit into the cuffs of his coat. He nodded agreement to the red-faced man, and smiled at the Deutschman and his wife. Jonathan wondered where the Ohio and big lake country were, and how many people it would take to fill up the country, especially if they kept coming so fast.

"Now, me," the red-faced man said, "I been here since me father came over from County Cashel,

Ireland, of course, lads. Sure, and ya knew that. There's too many people and too many buildings, horses, and smoke down there in Manhatten, or any of them towns there. I'm goin' west until I see nothin' but sky, and there's where I'll stay."

Jonathan politely asked, "How will you get there, sir?"

"Ah, lad, there's the mystery. I hear tell of big, flat boats made of logs that goes down the river to St. Louis, and then—well, I won't know til I get there. But, it'll be as green as home–not sooty like them big towns behind us there." He jerked his thumb back towards the east. "Oh, no." He clamped his square jaw shut.

A man, his wife, and their three little ones came down and sat about ten feet from Jonathan. An elderly lady passenger asked loudly, "Which is the best side to sit on?"

"It don't matter," shrugged the man near her.

The woman and her husband sat across from Jonathan. A young couple who were traveling with them sat down and began to chat noisily. More families with children came on board. Some were whining that they wanted to travel on the 'outside' of the boat, but parents quickly yanked them down the stairs to the dry innards of the boat. Jonathan felt more sad than ever in the presence of all these traveling families.

The boat gave a small shudder and the scenery started moving again. One of the older men opened a door in the bow which allowed fresh air to stream through the long cabin. A little girl ran up and down the aisle, bumping into passengers' legs.

Her mother called out, "Nora, oh Nora, come back here and sit down now!"

There was no break in the weather. Everyone stayed under cover of the roof most of the afternoon. It became very close and warm with body heat. Jonathan's nose told him which men near him worked with horses or cows. Everyone was grateful when someone occasionally opened the door in the bow to let in more fresh air.

Jonathan dozed in his bench seat. He was tired from getting up so early, but soon he became aware that the boat was stopping, and he saw the stonework of another lock. He heard some men laughing and saying that if this boat is the *Pride of Manlius*, it sure doesn't look to them like it was worth having any pride over. Jonathan didn't see any humor in the men's banter as he closed his eyes and soon dozed off again. When the boat slowed to a halt once more, some of the passengers were standing and getting ready to leave the boat.

Those who remained were moving out of the way so a crewman could set up the bunks for the night. Jonathan was looking out the window at the sights of Syracuse. He could see many larger stone buildings close to the canal. It seemed to him that this was a much larger town than Rome.

"Are you the lad who's bound for Weed's Basin?" the man asked.

Jonathan stirred from his deep sleep and wondered why he was being bothered in the middle of the night. He tried to crawl deeper into the blanket, but the man persisted.

"Son, you need to wake up and get off the boat. We're gonna be at the Basin soon."

Jonathan sleepily gathered his belongings and went up on deck, straining his eyes toward the quiet darkness ahead of the packet. Some other passengers were placing their own belongings in small piles at their feet, anticipating the rush to get close to the dock. He had only the cardboard suitcase to keep close. He felt anxious about meeting Uncle James, and didn't feel the urge to rush off the boat to meet someone he had seen only once or twice in his life. He thought it might be difficult to identify Uncle James, and he couldn't bear to think that he might not even be there to meet him.

CHAPTER SEVEN

A t last, in the early light of dawn, chimney smoke became visible above the trees, telling the passengers on deck that the village was near. The village lights told him that it was much smaller than Rome, but it looked to be a busy town. There were many businesses on the canal side and the basin itself was full of boats. The gang plank was hardly in place when people began to scurry off, their dark forms looking strange as they carried their unwieldy baggage down the gangplank. Some were being met by people they knew, while others looked one way and then the other as if they didn't know where they were going.

Jonathan started for the gangplank, urged on by the crew trying to get the boat on its way again so they could keep their schedule.

"Jonathan! Jonathan Hamilton!" A bearded man was waving and calling to him. "Here! Over here, boy. I'm your Uncle James."

Jonathan eyed the man carefully. He was not nearly as tall as his father, but he certainly resembled his mother, especially around the eyes—and the hair color was exactly as Jonathan remembered his mother's. He recalled that Uncle James was not quite two years older than his mother. He noted the short legs that made his arms seem a little too long. As Uncle James grabbed his hand to shake a welcome, he felt the strength in the hard-callused hand.

"How do you do, sir?" blurted Jonathan.

"Well, now, I'm fine, but don't call me sir. I was a sergeant, not an officer!" He laughed at his joke. "I'm your Uncle James. You and me—we're family!"

He gave Jonathan a big bear hug right there on the dock. Before Jonathan could recover, Uncle James had the cardboard suitcase and was a half-dozen steps toward town.

"Jonathan," he called over his shoulder, "C'mon, boy!"

As soon as Jonathan fell into step with his uncle, he listened with sadness to the story of how his Aunt Maude died, and how Uncle James needed a change from living in the house they shared for their ten years of marriage, and from where they had buried their two children as babies.

"The house isn't mine anymore—it only holds sorrow for me now." He went on to tell Jonathan he had put the farm up for sale right after Christmas, then the deal was made to rent it to a neighbor for a year rather than selling it. The cows and other livestock were sold, and Uncle James used the money to buy the canal boat.

"Well, almost all," Uncle James said. "I have a note at the bank, so I owe them a little," as he winked at Jonathan and smiled. "I did some trading of farm tools and such and swapped for paint and other such boating supplies—enough to paint the cabin–enough to make 'er stand out."

As Uncle James paused for breath, Jonathan quickly asked, "What color?"

The question interrupted Uncle James' line of thought, and it nearly slowed his walk to a halt. "White!" he said, regaining momentum. "White–and red for trim. With pots of 'ger-main-iums' on the cabin roof. What d'ya think?"

Jonathan thought *ger-RAIN-iums*, but before he could answer, Uncle James went on.

"Oh, yes, she'll be a beauty all right. Gotta scrape the old paint off first, then—you ever paint before? Well, no matter, you can be taught." He winked and grinned again as he switched the suitcase to his other hand.

"I'll carry it," Jonathan offered as he reached out for the suitcase.

"Never mind, I'm able. We'll be living on the boat, ya know, while we fix it up. Why, it'll be just like home —no by golly, it will be home." He poked the air with his free hand to emphasize the word. "There she is!" Uncle James picked up the pace in his excitement to show Jonathan the boat.

Even by the early morning light, he could see that the boat was scraped down to the bare wood in some places, and there were new boards here and there on the sides.

"The new boards are hemlock, and some of the cabin trim was replaced with nice beech I cut on the farm a few years ago. It dried out very well over the granary in the barn. I knew I'd need that wood for something. Your Aunt Maude said that if I had two barns I could fill them both with stuff I collect."

He winked, caught his breath again, and went on. "I didn't know much about fixing a boat proper-like, but I watched, asked questions, and learned how to use hemp—what they make rope out of—and white lead—what they make paint out of—and poked it into the cracks with an iron and a mallet. You know what a mallet is don't you? It's like one of your father's hammers, only the head's made of wood." He paused, tilted his head, squinted at Jonathan, and said, "Boy, I hope you're not dull-witted, because there's a lot to learn about canawling!"

Uncle James smiled, winked, and started toward the ladder propped against the canal boat as it sat in the mud. Jonathan looked for a drier way to get to the ladder than Uncle James, who just plodded straight through it. Uncle James looked over his shoulder, and said, "This dry dock isn't too dry, is it?" He smiled again, but didn't wink at Jonathan, who threw a scrap of board toward the ladder and carefully hopped on it and then to the bottom rung of the ladder.

Jonathan followed his uncle to the deck and toward the cabin at the rear of the boat. "I fixed up the living quarters first so I'd have a nice place to live while I fixed her up. Here's your bunk," as he dropped the suitcase on it. Jonathan thought it looked more like a box stall in a barn than a bed because of its construction.

The built-in bunk was enclosed with boards on the head and foot of the bed, and the far side was the outside wall of the boat. Jonathan would have to crawl over a side board to get into the bunk. Everything was clean and freshly painted, so it didn't really matter to him what the bunk looked like. Uncle James poked a couple of short pieces of wood into the still-hot stove, and took a black iron skillet from a nail in the galley wall.

"It's past breakfast time, so let's not waste too much time with it. I suppose you like bacon and eggs with a big chunk of bread and butter. Oh, the kitchen chores go like this: I cook and you clean up. Of course, if you're a good cook, I may have to clean up every once in awhile. Can you cook, Jonathan?" Uncle James asked with a twinkle in his eyes that Jonathan missed.

"No," Jonathan said ruefully.

He didn't want to do the dishes and pots all the time, but he'd never learned to cook. The fire heated up quickly, and soon the skillet crackled with the breakfast Uncle James was tending.

"Cut two fist-sized pieces of bread. It's in that cupboard." Uncle James pointed with the egg spatula, and said, "Your Uncle Jonas made this for your Aunt Maude years ago. Look at the stamp with his name on it." Jonathan saw the small brass filled letters 'J Hamilton' on the thin handle. It was the same kind of stamp that his father used to identify his own blacksmithing work.

By the time Jonathan sliced the bread, Uncle James was putting bacon and eggs into two thick blue dishes. Then he lifted the lid off a black pot and smelled the steam.

"Ahh, that's my stew." He jabbed a finger toward the stove. "I mostly drink tea—maybe you'll like it, too."

Jonathan picked up a fork, but Uncle James bowed his head, and prayed: "Thank you Father for Jonathan's safe journey here, and for this food. May it strengthen us for our labors. We pray in Jesus' name, Amen."

Jonathan felt a bit of confusion by the prayer. His parents had always been church-going, praying people; that is, until his mother died. His father stopped going then. He was pleased that his Uncle James was a praying man.

"Uncle James, will you show me how to prepare that stew—cutting the meat and carrots, and the rest? It smells like the stew my mother used to make."

"Well, takes practice," the older man smiled. "I will give you some lessons later. But for now, there are dirty dishes to wash. Jonathan got a lesson in heating up water and how to scrub the grease from dishes and skillet using hot water and a few chips of hard yellow lye soap.

When he finished that chore, he couldn't find Uncle James. He scanned the dry dock, and saw Uncle James with a mule and a wagon on the far side. He saw Jonathan, and waved him over.

"Gotta go to the farm and pick up some lumber, and you're the helper. Let's go."

They climbed up on the big freight wagon, and started out of the Basin. Not long after they left the edge of town, they pulled into the lane of a well-kept farm.

"This is—was—our place. Well, it still is mine, I expect. Smitty's only renting it. They moved into the house, 'cause it's better than theirs next door,' and he's farming both places. He's a hard worker, Jonathan."

All three spent over an hour sorting through the many boards stored in the hay mow and several out-buildings nearby. Jonathan also listened to the two men exchanging stories, discussing crops, and farm prices. Then they were invited to dinner, followed by a nap, before starting the chores and milking. Uncle James couldn't get away from the place without helping Smitty milk. Jonathan could see the love these men had for the animals.

That job completed, they headed back to the Basin, with Jonathan carefully holding a container of fresh milk, and another of pot roast with potatoes and carrots. After unloading the wagon, and carrying the lumber to the canal boat, they ate a light supper of leftovers.

Soon Uncle James asked Jonathan, "Does that bunk seem like a good idea?"

Uncle James didn't wait for an answer. He could see that the excitement and hard work of the day was beginning to show in Jonathan's tired eyes.

"Water's right here, and soap," he jabbed a stubby finger at the washstand. "Towel," he added, pointing to the bar that was attached to the stand.

"Hope you don't mind the light. I've got some reading to do." He turned and reached into a bookshelf that looked like Jonathan's bunk in miniature. Uncle James pulled out a well-worn, leather covered Bible. "I've been reading from the Proverbs. Do you ever read them?" he asked.

Jonathan was rubbing his face dry as he mumbled, "No sir, my mother did."

"Well, try this one on for size! 'Hear, ye children, the instruction of a father.'" Jonathan looked from behind his towel with one eye, not knowing how to respond. Finally, he could not hide behind the towel any longer.

"I'm very tired, Uncle James," he said. He stepped to the bunk and wiggled over the board on the edge. "Could we talk more tomorrow?" He rolled on his side, grabbed the covers, and turned away from the light. "G'night, Uncle James."

"Sleep well, Jonathan," came the reply. Uncle James sat closer to the yellow glow of the lantern and continued reading in the now quiet cabin.

CHAPTER EIGHT

Jonathan was awakened by the wonderful smell of bacon frying. He was ready to jump up to see what else there might be to eat for breakfast, but he hesitated. What if Uncle James had work planned for Jonathan before he could eat his breakfast? What if he had to cook his own breakfast?

Before he had a chance to worry about it for long, Uncle James stuck his head through the curtain and smiled a "Good morning!" and added, "C'mon, your eggs are getting cold."

Jonathan quickly pulled on his pants, and tucked in his shirt as he took the few steps to the combination galley and cabin. The room was warmed by the fire in the cook stove, and Jonathan lingered by the stove, warming his face. His eyes moved to the plate of bacon, eggs and biscuits, that were on the table by him. Uncle James had nearly finished his own breakfast, and jabbed a fork toward Jonathan's plate.

"C'mon, eat, we got a lot to do today."

"Yessir." Jonathan slid forward on the bench, but before he could get the fork into the eggs, Uncle James said, "You need to thank God for His provision."

"Yes sir, I will," returned Jonathan.

He bowed his head, and tried to remember the table prayers that his father used to say when his mother was alive. In his mind he stumbled through a prayer of thanks for the breakfast under his nose, and in a loud whisper he said, "Amen."

"Your father wrote in his letter that you're not afraid of work, and that you do chores around the house and shop. I'm sure glad that I don't have to teach you how to work!" He winked and smiled. "That will make it easier for the two of us to keep this cabin clean, and the cooking and dishwashing done. I mostly keep a pot of stew on the back of the stove, so that makes things simple. I buy bread, eggs, and fresh meat every few days, and there's bacon in that crock. Plenty of vegetables in the bin there." He paused for a breath and continued.

"We'll boil up our dirty clothes, and hang them out to dry, and a lot of other things that wives and mothers do. It's a necessity for us now," he said, as he reached over, squeezed Jonathan's arm, and smiled sadly. Jonathan nodded in agreement.

Uncle James suddenly stood up, and said, "So, you wash the dishes and sweep the cabin. I already put a pot of water on the stove for you to do the dishwashing, but you'll have to remember to do it from now on. I'll get the tools and materials ready—so when you're done in here, come out and be ready for a day's work." He turned as he went through the doorway and smiled, "You'll do fine, Jonathan."

Jonathan located all the cleaning materials and set to work at the tasks assigned to him. Although he didn't really like doing them, he felt that if Uncle James could do such work, then he could, too. He made sure he did the dishes better than they were done yesterday, and did a good job of sweeping–even in the corners and under the table. *Even my step-mother would like the job I've done,* he thought.

He brushed aside the thoughts of home and went out into the sunlight. Jonathan could hear sounds coming from all directions. One other boat shared the space in the muddy dry dock, and men were hard at work repairing its hull. Other canal boats were docked in the basin nearby and men and boys all rushed about carrying lumber or tools. Some were pushing, pulling, or carrying loads to and from the canal boats. It was exciting to be included as a worker on the great Erie Canal!

Jonathan heard the sound of muffled hammer-ing over the side of the canal boat. He saw Uncle James stuffing some strands of string in between the boat's boards, tapping it into place. He recognized the smell of linseed oil from its use in the blacksmith's shop. It was mixed with a whitish material, which Jonathan remembered was called lead.

"Uncle James, what do you want me to do?" he called out as he leaned over the rail.

Squinting up into the sunlight, Uncle James

looked at Jonathan. "Come on down here, and see how to do this," he said as he motioned with the ball of string.

Jonathan quickly backed down the ladder and stood with Uncle James on a scrap of wide planking.

"This oil and lead is pretty nasty stuff to get into, so watch your clothes. Roll up your sleeves real good, so they won't come down and get into this stuff. I want you to squeeze this into these lengths of hemp—that's rope to you, I suspect. Then hand them to me and I'll cork up these joints in the boards."

Soon Jonathan was doing his best to squeeze the mixture into the stringy lines of hemp. After an hour, the muscles in his forearms ached from the task, and he longed for a rest. Cranking the bellows in the blacksmith shop didn't require the same muscles that this required. Uncle James noticed Jonathan stretching his arms and trying to ease the cramps. He suggested that he could rub his hands on a piece of hemp to clean them up some, and they would sit and rest a bit.

Jonathan sat on a stool with his arms spread out to keep the oily mixture from getting on his clothing. He looked down at his shirt front and trousers to see how much of a mess he had made of his clothing. He was surprised to see only one thin line of oil where a length of hemp had escaped his grasp.

Uncle James broke the silence. "That linseed oil will start a fire just like damp hay in a haymow. So, you need to scrub it out with turpentine, let it dry some, and wash it good with lye soap. You're doing all right, Jonathan—a good worker. But, we have to get back at it." He stood up and stretched. "We have to keep up with the crew working on this boat next to us, because when it's done, They're lettin' the water back into this dry dock, which means we have to be ready to float."

After another long period of work, it was time for the noon meal.

"Dinnertime," was all Uncle James said. The older man wiped his hands on a rag, and carefully draped it over a board so that it would have plenty of air to keep it from heating up. Jonathan followed the example, and they climbed the ladder to the boat deck.

Jonathan's arms ached so much that he was sure he wouldn't be able to lift the food to his mouth. As Uncle James noticed, it was not the case. Jonathan ate like he had not eaten for a long time, and with no problem with his arms. It was Uncle James' turn to do the dishes, and he suggested that Jonathan might like to rest in his bunk for a while. Jonathan smiled in gratitude, and was behind the curtain in no time.

Soon enough, both were heading back down the ladder and back at the task. All afternoon they worked at sawing and planing several boards to replace some rotted ones. Uncle James was very meticulous in planing off small amounts of wood, then checking for fit. He said the wood will swell up some, making it watertight even without the application of hemp and caulk.

To keep the wood from splitting when it was nailed to the side, small holes were drilled in the ends of all the new boards. Jonathan used the breast drill for that task, following the instructions from Uncle James.

"Don't need any broken drill bits. You know all the money blacksmiths get when they make tools."

Before Jonathan could begin to defend his father's trade, he saw the twinkle, and the beginnings of a smile.

Jonathan nodded and replied, "Oh, yes sir, way too much money."

They laughed at their jokes. Jonathan drilled the small holes, keeping ahead of Uncle James as he placed the boards and carefully drove in the nails.

"Oh, she's looking better and better!" smiled Uncle James. "Another day and she'll be ready to float. Then we'll have to do some painting topside. Uncle James leaned back on the canal boat, rubbed his hands together, and looked at his palms, checking for sawdust. Satisfied that they passed inspection, he looked at Jonathan. "What do you know about mules? Have you ever had reins in your hands—driven a team of horses or mules?"

Jonathan looked at his shoes. "No, sir, I never." He answered quietly.

"Well, some people think mules are pretty dumb, ornery creatures, but mine are pretty smart. They like me and I like them. My farmer friend, Smitty, is bringing them over from the farm this evening. We'll get acquainted and we'll see about working together."

Jonathan was still looking at his shoes, but from the sound of Uncle James's voice he knew that

Uncle James was smiling. He looked up into Uncle James's eyes.

"They're really quite pleasant and obedient," the man said softly.

Some time later, Jonathan heard heavy hooves pounding the hard ground, coming closer to the basin where the two canal boats were being repaired. He stood up from his task at the same time Uncle James came out of the cabin.

"Hello, Smitty," Uncle James shouted.

Tied to the back of the farmer's wagon were two large, light brown mules. Smitty climbed down from the wagon.

"Here's your babies!" he said with a smile. Both men laughed.

"I thank you. They're looking very good," Uncle James returned. He walked over to the team and they leaned toward Uncle James. "Hello, Hezekiah, hello Deuteronomy."

Jonathan cocked his head, and with a smile asked, "What did you call them? Are those real names?"

Uncle James smiled at Jonathan and reached for the nearest mule's nose.

He said, "How's my Hezzy?" and rubbed and petted the mule's nose.

The other mule strained to get closer in order to get some attention, too. Uncle James reached over the first mule's head and began the same treatment for the second mule.

"Well, Deut, you need some loving, too?"

He turned to Jonathan, "Come on, son, let me introduce you to my hard workers. Jonathan, meet Deuteronomy. And this is Hezekiah."

Jonathan reached up and gingerly touched the soft nose.

He wanted to ask, "Will it bite?" but instead exclaimed, "It's so soft."

Hezakiah leaned towards Jonathan as if to say 'More', so Jonathan reached up and rubbed the soft nose again.

The boy smiled, "Hello Hezzy," he said. Then he reached over and repeated the rubbing, "Hello, Deut." Deuteronomy responded by exhaling his warm breath in Jonathan's direction.

Uncle James was watching the boy and the mules.

He said, "I think you'll get along just fine. They're really quite docile and they do what they're told. You won't have any problems. We'll do some training, and you'll be used to each other in no time."

He untied the halters and led the mules towards the Deliverance. He turned to Smitty who had climbed back into his wagon seat.

"Thanks Smitty. Say hello to the missus."

"Sure, I'll do that. Goodbye, Jimmy." He clucked at his team, swung them around, and trotted them from the Basin.

Jonathan caught up to his fast-walking uncle and asked, "May I take one?"

Uncle James thought for a second or so and handed the rope to Jonathan. "You have Hezzy. See the white star between the eyes? Now look at Deut. The white marking on his nose is longer."

Jonathan looked at Deut, then at Hezzy. Again he looked back at the mules and then he nodded. "I've got that. Now, how about driving mules? That's probably harder to learn," he said to his Uncle with a slightly worried look on his face.

Uncle James waved a hand, "Ah, you'll get it as easily as corking and painting. Remember, you have a good teacher." He thrust his head back and laughed, "And I have a smart student."

Later, back at work on the canal boat, Uncle James was right in his guess of how long it would take to complete the boards and the messy corking with oil and lead. Soon both were working on the painting. It was hard work lying on their backs in the mud to paint the very bottom—the keel—of the boat. Then they were able to sit on a stool to spread the paint on the boards. There was little time for talking, but Uncle James came over a few times to make sure the paint was going on smoothly, and that there were no missed spots.

Later, as they rested on their stools, Jonathan asked, "How long will it take this paint to dry?"

"A day or two, depending on how hot and muggy it gets," came Uncle James' reply. "We can finish painting the top part when she's in the water, but this hull must be dry!" He waved a spotty white hand toward the boat.

Uncle James' estimate was right again. By late afternoon of the second day, the paint was dry to the touch, and it looked as good as any paid artisan might have done.

"Captain McManus. Are you ready, sir?" A man carrying a lantern called from the darkening canal bank. "We aim to float the boats at first light."

"Yes, indeed, we are!" Uncle James stood up and shouted in the direction of the lantern light. "Send in the water!" Then he put his arm around Jonathan and said, "We're ready, with God's help, aren't we?"

He paused, turned towards the ladder, and said to Jonathan, "C'mon up, I want to show you something."

Once in the cabin, Uncle James reached into a cupboard, brought out a carved and painted board, and proudly showed Jonathan the boat's nameplate: *The Deliverance.*

CHAPTER NINE

"Mr. James McManus! Are you Mr. James McManus?"

Jonathan quickly turned from his deck work to see who was calling for Uncle James. He stared at the thin, dark-haired boy who stood on the bank of the dry dock. After coming on board, the newly-named *Deliverance*, the boy shyly said hello and quickly produced a letter of introduction from a Mr. Cartwright, a man Uncle James knew in Montezuma, a village west of Weed's Basin.

Uncle James read the letter out loud. It said that this boy, Charles Smith, would be honest and hard-working for whoever hired him. It also said that the writer hoped Uncle James would need a boy to help him, because this boy needed some good direction and up-bringing.

Uncle James closed his eyes for a moment, looked at Charles and said, "I'll try you for a week, then I will better know if you are able to work for me for the whole season."

After their supper and the evening chores around the boat were done, the boys settled into their bunks and exchanged stories for some time before they settled off to sleep. Each night they shared more about their young lives, and as the stories unfolded, each boy gained respect for the other. Jonathan was very impressed by Charles' tale of what happened to him a year ago. Charles was orphaned at the age of eight, and was put to work on a line boat as a bailer. He pumped out the water that leaked into the bottom of the boat so it wouldn't come high enough to soak the floorboards.

Next, he was taken in by a tavernkeeper who kept him much like a slave, sweeping, washing dishes and mugs, shoveling snow, feeding stock, and running errands. He received no pay, and only scraps and leftovers to eat. He slept in the stable with the stock. Because Charles was tall for his age, most people thought he was older and he was able to get a paying job on a cargo boat driving mules. Near the end of July, Charles became very sick with chills and dizziness. The captain would not let him back on the boat, or give him any remedies for his illness. As he continued to drive the team, he became so weak and lightheaded that he fell down and hit his head so hard that he passed out there on the towpath.

The bad-tempered captain dragged Charles into a shack near the canal lock and left him there. The lock-tender was as bad a man as the captain, and did nothing to help.

Whenever anyone questioned him about the boy in the shack, he told people, "That evil boy is better off dead. He is the worst boy on the canal."

Charles lay in the shack for the rest of the day. About dusk, a passenger on a canal boat who happened to be Mr. Cartwright, jumped off the boat, and according to Charles, was just like the good Samaritan.

The lock tender gave such a heartless response that the man said, "I don't know that he is dead, but if he is alive I shall try to save him."

Charles was placed in a cart and taken to a doctor who cared for his wounds. Mr. Cartwright and his wife cared for Charles all through the winter, and he gradually re-gained his health and strength. He stayed with them until the day he came to ask Uncle James for a job. He told Jonathan that since his own parents died, he had never been treated with such kindness. He was also given good advice which Charles said he planned to put to use. Charles was told to seek out Godly men to work for, and to go to school when he wasn't working on the canal. Charles told Jonathan that he would follow that advice and maybe someday he could be the captain of a boat, or even the owner of a boat line.

At supper time, Uncle James pulled the *Deliverance* over to the bank and Jonathan unhitched the mules. He and Charles drove the mules up the planks and into the boat's stable where they were given fresh water, hay, and grain. The boys shook out some fresh straw for bedding, and headed for the cabin. Uncle

James called the boys into the galley where he gave them a lesson on making that wonderful beef stew. The pleasing aroma from the stew soon encouraged both Jonathan and Charles to move quickly. As they worked together, they heard a shout from the canal side.

"James! I say James, will you give hospitality to a brother in the Lord?"

Both boys stopped and looked at each other with a questioning expression on their faces.

CHAPTER TEN

"James!" The deep voice echoed again in the quiet evening air on the canal side.

"Huh!" Uncle James jumped up from his bench seat. "That sounds like Deacon Eaton! Boys, we're in for some good company tonight."

The boys heard the two men noisily greeting each other in the twilight as Uncle James extended the gangplank over the side for the man standing on the canal bank. Uncle James and the boys went through the cabin doorway easily, but the stranger filled the door opening, and even had to duck until he slid himself into the bench on the other side of the table.

"Deacon Eaton, I would have you meet two fine boys. They are with me at present on this new venture of mine on the Grand Canal." He pointed with his big hand across the table to Jonathan. "This is my late sister's son, Jonathan Hamilton, and this is our new friend Charles Smith. This lad has seen far worse days than any of the three of us. But, the good Lord has seen fit to deliver him from those past afflictions."

"Amen to that!" said Deacon Eaton.

The visitor smiled broadly, showing a full set of large straight teeth. His graying hair was thinning on his large head, and his hands were not those the boys expected to see on this preacher. Instead, they looked like those of a man who worked long and hard for his living. His suit was somewhat dusty from the path, but it had sharp creases at the collar and sleeves. Deacon Eaton was obviously pleased to see Uncle James, and the two men lost no time talking about the weather or crops, but immediately were deep in conversation.

"Your dear wife Maude," he lingered over her name, "she has gone to be with the Lord, as has this lad's mother?" Uncle James' face softened as he nodded.

It looked to Jonathan from across the table that tears were welling up in his uncle's eyes.

"Yes," Uncle James said softly. "Ellen passed on first, then my own dear Maude—just seven weeks before Jonathan arrived in Weed's Basin to join me in this work for the summer. I cared for her during her illness all during spring planting so I had no crops in the ground. I was glad to rent the farm to my neighbor, Smitty, who is a hard worker. Then, this canal boat became available just at the right moment for me. It keeps my heart from grieving so by keeping me busy."

"Could we pray about this right now?" asked the Deacon.

"Oh, yes, please do," smiled Uncle James.

Both men bowed their heads and closed their eyes. The Deacon prayed for strength and protection for Uncle James, Jonathan, and Charles. The boys looked at each other, both surprised and encouraged by the strong devotion that was so obviously present in these men.

"Well, my boys," Uncle James began as the prayer was over, "The Deacon and I have much to talk about. You'd better get to your bunks. You have a long day ahead of you tomorrow."

Jonathan and Charles quickly got up from the table, said their goodnights, and went to their bunks beyond the curtain at the other side of the cabin. Jonathan motioned to Charles to keep silent as they got ready for bed. He didn't want to miss any of the talk between the two men. There was much he wanted to hear from the missionary's mouth as well as from Uncle James'.

"We heard from our friend in Montezuma that you started your missionary work on the canal over three years ago. You must have some interesting stories to tell," Uncle James said to his friend.

"Indeed I do, sir!" exclaimed the missionary. "When I first began on the canal, I would just walk onto a boat—a packet boat, that is, as a passenger. Then, I would go to see the captain and ask his permission to talk and pray with the crew and passengers. Then I would leave literature with them and get off at the next town. I would then repeat the process with the next packet arriving at that town. Sometimes the captain would agree to this and sometimes not."

"One captain said to me, 'I have been on the canal for twelve years, and you, sir, are the first man I have seen or heard of on the canal as a missionary. Church people have no objection to sending missionaries to the heathen world, but when we think of how long the canal has been in operation, and no thought taken for us, we have concluded that no man cared for our souls. I am very glad to see you, and you shall have all privileges while on my boat.'

"But it is the boys, James," the missionary continued, "toward whom I know the Lord is directing me with the most fervor. There are, at any one time, some 5,000 boys working on the canal. Half of them are orphans. The most money they can make for the season is $70.00. And the kind of weather we have in this part of central New York between April and October! Here those boys are—out in the weather—many times all through the night in rain, wind or even ice.

"Many a captain, James, does not profess Christianity as honestly as you do. Some of these men are ruthless and will cheat a boy out of a whole season's wages by treating him so badly in the last month of hire that the boy runs away." Deacon Eaton leaned over the table toward Uncle James. "James, I heard of a horrible incident. Last year one poor lad was beaten black and blue during the last month the canal was open. He went to the captain and said he needed to get back to his family in western New York. He asked for his wages, but the captain refused, and even denied the boy the chance to come back on board to get his belongings.

"Overnight the weather took very cold, and in the morning there was snow on the ground. He knew he had to get a coat or blanket if he was to survive the walk back to his father's farm. He made it to the nearest town, where he went into the nearest tavern, and when he thought no one was looking, he slipped a coat off a hook and made off with it.

"But someone did see him, and he was caught and placed in jail until he went before a local judge who sent him to the Auburn Prison for three years! I have visited the boy and will do so again when I am in Auburn.

"An incredible story, eh, James? Tell me, how is it that you have this lad—ahh, Charles, is it, here with you? What is the background of the boy? And how does this all fit in with your nephew Jonathan?"

At hearing their names mentioned, both boys stretched up on their elbows to hear more clearly. The boys heard Uncle James take a deep breath.

"I have a friend in Montezuma; a man I know and trust. He sent Charles to me and he has high hopes that Charles is on the road to becoming a fine man. As it says in Proverbs, 'Train up a child in the way he should go, and when he is old he will not depart from it.'

"A week ago when Charles came, I told him that I would be trying him out for a week. Deacon, I've not heard one foul word come out of that boy's mouth! And we both know that many of the canal orphans do use vile words. He has quickly learned to obey orders, and to work hard at the jobs I've given him to do. I will be keeping him with me as he's a boy I can trust, along with my nephew Jonathan.

"As you know, I serve the Lord in more mysterious ways than you do, and I must have workers who can be counted on."

Jonathan slowly slumped down on his arm as sleep began to overtake him. He was happy to learn that Charles would be staying with them, and that Uncle James thought highly of both boys. He wondered what Uncle James meant by 'serving the Lord in mysterious ways.' He would try to remember to ask Uncle James about that. As the men's voices droned on, slow breathing filled the boy's end of the cabin.

CHAPTER ELEVEN

A long day passed slowly for the boys. Each led the mules for two hours, and then the other took his turn. Now, Jonathan tightened his grip on the reigns as he walked along the towpath behind the mules. Daylight was beginning to fade, and the air was hot, humid, and uncomfortable to him. Flies and mosquitoes continued to pester both the mules and the boatmen. Jonathan pulled his hat closer to the back of his collar, and at the same time tried to pull the brim down to keep the mosquitoes from his face, but the hat wasn't big enough.

He switched the reins from left hand

to right as he pulled his sleeves down and buttoned them—all this done within the constant rhythm of 'the walk.'

"There must be more swamp land in central New York than in all the jungles of Africa," mumbled Jonathan to himself.

It hardly seemed possible that he had been fighting this persistent mosquito battle since that first day he began walking in late May. The sound of his name being shouted from the *Deliverance* brought him back from his thoughts.

"Jonathan, we're picking up cargo in Camillus. Turn down the feeder path," his Uncle shouted. "Keep goin' 'til we get to the dock."

"That's strange," Jonathan whispered. "Camillus? And to keep driving when it's getting dark.... I wonder what we're picking up there."

His thinking aloud was suddenly interrupted. A great blue heron was startled from where it stood fishing at the edge of the canal. Its huge wings flapped by the surprised Hezekiah the mule who lurched into the path of his partner Deuteronomy. Jonathan held tight to the reins and calmed the mules.

Jonathan could see up ahead to the turn-off. The feeder would leave the Erie and go a mile or so south to the village of Camillus, thus connecting another small central New York town to the great waterway. This length seemed to have more mosquitoes buzzing about so he knew he would have to pay close attention to his driving, especially with the daylight fading so fast. The mules didn't like being bitten any more than he did.

As they neared the village, Jonathan knew that Charles would be ready to jump to shore, and slip the thick rope around the large post planted deep in the ground. The friction of the tightened rope against the post would act as a brake to stop the boat's forward motion. Then Jonathan and Charles would place the long ropes around posts to keep the canal boat in place for loading the cargo.

Once the boat was tied up, Jonathan watered the mules and the boys looked around the small dock area. Jonathan noticed a large freight wagon with several barrels on it being driven down the road adjacent to the canal. The driver reined his team in alongside the *Deliverance*. Uncle James had the gangplank placed by the time the wagon came to a complete stop. The teamster was down off his rig in a flash and just as quickly had the team tied. Jonathan and Charles stood admiring the six-horse hitch.

"What's in the barrels?" asked Charles.

Jonathan just shrugged his shoulders, as Uncle James started to help unload the barrels from the wagon, and to carefully roll them onto the *Deliverance*.

"Just keep back, boys, this here's men's work!" The teamster grinned at the boys. Then in a kinder voice, he said "These barrels are hard to roll straight."

It only took a few minutes for the barrels to be loaded, and Uncle James and the teamster disappeared into the cabin for a few minutes.

As they came up on deck, Uncle James called the boys to action. "Wake those mules, boys, and let's see if we can turn this boat around without breaking the canal banks."

The teamster laughed at the comment and shouted from the wagon seat, "You'll have to hit 'er pretty hard, Brother McManus."

Charles untied both lines holding the boat and hopped aboard, leaving Jonathan alone with the mules, heading north toward the Erie. After a quarter hour of walking through the deserted stretch of towpath, he was sure he could hear voices talking and laughing. He thought he heard Uncle James, too. Jonathan looked to either side for the light of some house in the area, but there were no houses. He turned again toward the *Deliverance.* Jonathan was sure he could hear men and women talking. He shook his head in disbelief. *I must be imagining things*, he thought.

The sound of the horn startled Jonathan. His uncle blew the conch horn to warn the lock tender of their approach. Jonathan was not paying attention, and was surprised to see the lock so close. The sound of voices had stopped some time ago, and his empty stomach took a lot of his attention. His shoulders and back muscles needed attention, too. He knew that while they were going through the lock, Uncle James would want the teams and drivers exchanged. After he cared for the mules, giving them feed, water, and a good rubdown, it would be his turn for food and a good rest.

As Charles brought his team off the boat, he passed Jonathan with a broad smile on his face. "Hurry with your team and get to the cabin!" was all he said as he passed by his friend.

Jonathan muttered a question to Charles, but he disappeared in the dark without a further explanation. The stable tasks completed, he made his way to the cabin. He hesitated at the door, which opened suddenly, and Uncle James pulled the bewildered boy inside. He looked around the small room in surprise, because seated at the table were dark-faced men and women. Two black boys squatted together on the deck.

"What, who are..." Jonathan stopped, at a loss for words.

Uncle James smiled, and calmly answered, "These good folks, recently from northern Virginia, are headed for Canada." He paused, and continued. "This is a part of our lives that Maude and I never shared with the rest of the family, Jonathan. It's been a while since I've helped anyone to get north, in what some people call the 'Underground Railroad.' I can't ask you to approve of what I do, but since you've come into my care, I'll expect you to help Charles and me keep them safe and speed them on their journey. No matter how you feel, you must never tell anyone about this." Silence filled the cabin as they stared at each other.

"Well..." Jonathan's voice broke the long silence. "I love you, Uncle James, and...." He paused, stumbling for the right words. "I trust you, and I...I hope you trust me, because I want to be...a helper."

He finished his stilted comments with a big sigh of relief, and Uncle James said, "I thought you would. Thank you."

The black man sitting next to Uncle James got up and motioned for Jonathan to sit at the table, while

Uncle James slid out of the bench seat and dipped a portion of stew for Jonathan. As Jonathan sat down, his eyes took in the dark group seated in the cabin. He counted two men and two women squeezed into the benches at the table, and the two boys seated on the floor near the stove.

"Our main job," Uncle James said, "is to see that these folks get from here to Oswego and onto a ship that will take them across the lake to Kingston. Right now, the roads are being watched pretty close, but these folks need to get through now!" He dropped his big open hand on the table top for emphasis, just missing Jonathan's stew plate. "I suppose it would surprise people to know this 'railroad' sometimes goes by water!"

Several smiles now brightened the room at the small joke, and the tension again left the cabin. "Just in case we have some un-wanted visitors, we have to see that the Brown family here can disappear mighty quick. I want to show you something I built into the boat before you came aboard." Uncle James opened the door between the cabin and the hold, started toward the stalls, and motioned for them to follow. "Jonathan, see this board with the big knot? Watch!" He pushed the wide board near the top, and it swung aside, revealing a long black hallway.

CHAPTER TWELVE

onathan strained his eyes to see further, and he was able to make out a space about a foot and a half wide by eight feet long, and not quite six feet high. Uncle James started an explanation. "I hope we don't have to use this 'hidey hole, folks," said Uncle James, "but in case we should be stopped, you'll be safe and sound in there. You'll have to stand up in that narrow space—no room to sit—but it'll be safe!"

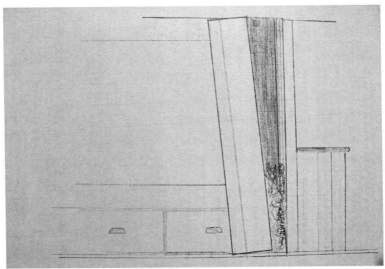

Jonathan was amazed! He looked at the grain bin wall, then back to the inside of the hidey hole, as if to measure the wall in his mind. He smiled and shook his head like someone just caught in a joke. "Great work, Uncle James! It's really hidden."

Uncle James smiled. "Thank you, Jonathan." He continued his explanation. "There's more. We have a signal bell—it's tied to a string and strung through holes drilled in the braces behind the wallboards. You can stay in the cargo area, or rest on the straw in the stall, but if there are any signs of danger, we'll pull the string and into the hidey hole you go. The last one in pushes the board and slides this bar into place. Then it can be opened only from the inside." He paused for a breath, smiled, and added, "Don't worry, there's plenty of good air in there, like a summer breeze." He swept the air with his arm for emphasis.

There were smiles and nods from the Browns. "We got it, Brudder McManus. Thank you."

"Now, it's time for all of you to bed down for the night. Just spread yourselves out on the straw here. Have a restful night." Jonathan and Uncle James returned to the cabin of the *Deliverance.*

"Uncle James?" Jonathan questioned.

"Yes, Jonathan, what is it?" Uncle James replied.

Jonathan hesitated and looked down at the table. He didn't know how to ask the questions going through his mind without troubling his uncle.

"I would imagine that you'd like to know how I became involved with the 'Railroad'," he said.

"Yes," Jonathan answered quietly.

Silence filled the cabin. Neither spoke for what seemed a long time. At last, Uncle James cleared his throat, as if preparing his voice for a struggle.

"Your grandfather had a saying Jonathan," he began. "It does no good to feel strongly about a matter and do nothing about it. Your mother and I heard our father say that many times. So many times, in fact, that we believed it to be the truth. When I came to this country, I saw slavery as evil. I felt strongly about it. I wondered what I, an immigrant, could do about it. When your Aunt Maude and I married, I told her that I had to take action on the issue of slavery.

"When we took over her father's farm after his death, we built a secret room into the center of the second floor of the farm house. We reasoned that since very few people ever visited the farm, much less went up the stairs, they'd never realize that the center of the second floor had been tampered with. We found out that we could be a 'station' on the 'railroad' quite by accident. Some black folk who were escaping from slavery in the South took a wrong turn and ended up at our farm. We hid them that night in our secret room. They journeyed along, eventually finding the right 'station' and let those people know about us. From then on, we were part of the 'railroad.' Your Aunt Maude made me promise only one thing as she was dyin'; that I would continue with helping our black brothers and sisters.

"It's a bad business, Jonathan," Uncle James continued. "Oh, I know, there's always been more white slaves than black ones when you look back over the history of the world. But here, in this country, the blacks were captured from their homeland and then forced into slavery. The whites in this country who indentured themselves did so by agreement. That means they have to work long and hard for many years for the owner of their 'papers', but they do see an opportunity for freedom. It is a rare black man or woman who has a master who will consider freedom for their 'people' as they like to call their slaves. You mark my words, Jonathan, even if slavery were to come to an end tomorrow, this injustice will cause problems for black people and white people for years and years to come. This country will not see these problems go away for many years."

Uncle James paused in his speaking, and Jonathan slowly said, "I have another question, Uncle James."

"Well, go ahead and ask it. There's no secrets between you and me."

"Uncle James," Jonathan paused, not sure how to ask. "Well, what makes you so different? My Pa and you both lost their wives, but you don't act like him. Pa, well, Pa got mean after Ma died. He's still angry a lot. You don't act like that—you act, well, you act happy and joyful and I know that you're sad that you lost Aunt Maude. How can you be joyful?"

There was silence in the cabin for a long minute. The older man's eyes filled with tears and he stood up. He looked off in the distance, and reached up to the shelf that held his books. He grasped the worn leather Bible and placed it on the table between them.

"It's all in here, son," he murmured. "I'm no missionary like Deacon Eaton, so maybe I can't tell you so well myself, but the story you need to know is in here. Let me read you a bit, and then I'll show you where to read more by yourself."

Uncle James quickly thumbed to the book he was looking for, and said, "There are many places in the Bible that I could use to tell you about Jesus. Your mother and I had a Godly mother and father who read the Bible to us every day. One night what he was reading to us it just made sense to me. Here's the verses that helped me understand how important it is for us to know God–personal like.

"This is from Paul's letter to the Romans, Jonathan. Let me try to put it into words that you can understand. 'That if you confess with your mouth 'Jesus is Lord' and believe in your heart that God raised him from the dead, you will be saved. For it is with your heart that you believe and are justified and it is with your mouth that you confess and are saved.' As the Scripture says, 'Anyone who trusts in Him will never be put to shame.'

"You see, Jonathan, our father read those Bible stories to us, all those great stories about Noah, David, Abraham; and how Jesus was born in a barn, and how He grew up. He told us how Jesus died for us so we could be forgiven by God and be in His heavenly kingdom when we die. I didn't understand what I had to do to have that joy in my heart, the joy you see in me, Jonathan. I tried to be good, oh I tried, but I knew that I could never be good enough for God. So, I prayed and asked God to show me how I could be His. When Father started to read this letter to the Romans, it all started to make sense. I talked to my father and he said I was on the right road. Before long, I did confess that 'Jesus is Lord' and soon I had my own Bible so I could read God's truth for myself. By doing that, I feel close to Him and I know that He is where my joy comes from. But you're right, I do miss your Aunt Maude." He sighed, and went on. "I do know that she is with Jesus and that makes me glad."

Jonathan was silent. He wasn't surprised at his Uncle's answer. He was pretty sure that the old, worn Bible on the table between them would be a large part of the reason for the difference in Uncle James.

"Uncle James, would you start to read your Bible out loud to Charles and me at night?"

Uncle James smiled as he answered. "I'll be happy to share the Word with you two. I should have done it before." He pointed a stubby finger toward Jonathan.

"In your bunk, boy! It won't be long before you have to go out and relieve Charles. We'll not stop until we reach Oswego!" Uncle James said, sounding just like a politician promising something in a speech.

Jonathan nodded and made his way back toward his bunk. He now knew that there was a group of people living in several states who helped former slaves escape from the southern states to the north or to Canada. This 'underground railroad' was connected by safe houses that had hidden closets or spaces behind walls where the black people could be hidden during the day, and guided by night to the next stop on the railroad. Although the long evening had been full of surprises and excitement, he was suddenly very tired, and happy to be getting in the bunk. He needed no covers on him this hot night, and despite the excitement, he made a choice to stop and kneel beside his bunk.

"Dear God," he said quietly, "this has been quite a day for us. Please be with us tomorrow and help us get the Browns to the ship safely. And God, please help me to know you in the way that Uncle James does. Amen."

He lifted himself over the edge of the bunk. He was soon breathing in a steady rhythm that told he was fast asleep.

CHAPTER THIRTEEN

The next morning Jonathan was out of his bunk early, and sleepily relieved Charles on the towpath. The *Deliverance* moved slowly northward on the canal, with the two young drivers keeping a wary eye out for the 'unwanted visitors' Uncle James warned about earlier. Each time the boys changed shifts, and cared for the mules, two slender black boys, close to their own ages, stood silently outside the stall and watched. It seemed to Jonathan that the boys were interested in more than the mules, and probably wanted to talk with him.

Jonathan suddenly looked up, and asked, "You used to mules?"

Both heads bobbed up and down at once. Encouraged, Jonathan then asked, "Your daddy got mules?"

The two boys stood frozen in place, staring silently at Jonathan. He immediately realized that the question showed his ignorance, and he felt his face turn hot with embarrassment.

He stammered, "Well, I guess I forgot where you're comin' from." He grimaced, looked away, and said "I'm sorry."

He spit out the apology quickly as he brushed the straw chaff from his hands.

He tried another question that he was sure he couldn't cause himself embarrassment.

"Are you hungry? I sure am!" The heads bobbed again. "Well, come up to the cabin. Uncle James always has a pot of stew on the stove. Jonathan led the way to the cabin, with the two young hideaways right behind him. Jonathan motioned for both boys to sit down, and took three bowls from the dish cupboard.

As he ladled the darkened vegetables and thick beef broth into the bowls, he said, "There are spoons in that cubby hole by the table." He smiled and asked "What are your names?"

The boy closest to him placed three spoons on the table and nodded to the boy next to him. "This here's Zeke, and my name be Zack. We got Bible names jus' like you." He said this with an assured voice, not one of pride or arrogance.

It seemed to Jonathan that having a Biblical name meant a great deal to Isaac, so he asked, "Do you know much about the Bible?" he asked.

Again both heads bobbed together, this time with big smiles. "Our ol' massa," Isaac said slowly, "were a good man. He knew de Lawd. He made sure his darkies got to hear 'bout Jesus."

"Then why did you run away?" Jonathan interrupted. "Why didn't you stay there with him?"

"Massa died," Ezekiel said flatly. "Daddy said the white folks got to fightin' 'bout sellin' the whole place, house, land, and us, too. The ol' massa, he good to us. We live wid our fam'lies, mommas, daddies, and children. Mos' massas don't 'low dat. Our daddies say we bes' get outta dere 'for dat happen to us."

The shock of the story showed on Jonathan's face, as he cut three slabs of Johnnycake from the iron skillet, and put a piece next to each steaming bowl. The three boys ate in silence, because of their hunger, and because they did not know what else to say. The lantern in the cabin lit their solemn faces as they ate.

Jonathan studied their faces as he noticed some similarities, and he asked, "You two brothers?"

"Naw," answered Isaac. "Our mommas is sisters. Their momma come from Affika–and our ol' massa, he bought our daddies."

"They done jumped de broom!" Zeke added proudly.

Jonathan never heard that phrase before. "What does that mean, 'jump the broom'?" he asked.

"Slaves don't have no proppa weddin' like white folks. Dey jus' jump de broom."

He held both hands palms up, as if to show how simple it was. Jonathan was still unsure of the meaning, so moved to another question.

"What do slaves do?" he asked.

"Dey do what de massa tell 'em to do," said Isaac, with a serious face.

"Dey does all de work," added Ezekiel, with a nod for emphasis.

"Were there many slaves on the farm where you lived?" Jonathan questioned.

"Yeah, dey was a lot of us, I guess. I don't know no numbers, so's I don't know for a fac'."

Jonathan paused to consider that answer, and then asked, "How did you get away?"

"Oh, we didn't all go together," Isaac said. "We sneaked away one or two at a time," he continued.

Zeke quickly whispered a caution. "You said 'nuff, Zack."

Isaac nodded, and turned to look at Jonathan squarely, and said evenly, "We had a right hard time to get this far, and it won't be done 'til we's in Canada."

Jonathan didn't speak. He looked at Isaac first, then at Ezekiel, and got up from the table.

"I'll wash up the dishes, then I've got to get to bed. It's a long haul to Oswego. Mebbee you should get back to your folks."

"Sho'nuff," smiled Isaac. "We kin talk 'nutha time."

CHAPTER FOURTEEN

Jonathan's uncle was firmly shaking his shoulder.

"Wake up, boy," he said softly. "I need your help. We'll be locking through in a little while."

Jonathan felt that he had been asleep only for a short time, but he arose from the bunk and pulled his boots on. He was on deck quickly, looking ahead to the lock which was covered with misty darkness. Only the lock tender's lanterns gave out an eerie light in the blackness. The water looked dark and deep below him although he knew that a man could easily stand in the canal with his head above water. As they pulled into the lock, Jonathan was ready to tie the canal boat securely while Charles led the mules on the side.

Jonathan was fully awake now. He remembered the hidden Brown family down below. He felt his heart pumping faster with excitement. Uncle James came up from below.

"I've just told them to be very quiet from now on." He spoke evenly and softly. "I didn't tell you before,

Jonathan, but back at Camillus, the teamster told me that he was almost caught by two men on horseback. They are hunting for the people we have below. You must be very alert. Watch out for anything that doesn't look right. Toss this stone on the deck if you see two horsemen."

"Yes sir," Jonathan blurted.

He grasped the stone tightly in his fist as Uncle James moved out of sight into the foggy darkness. Jonathan knew it would be at least an hour to Syracuse and the junction of the Oswego Canal, but he had no idea of how far Oswego was. He felt very alone there as he stood on the upper deck of the *Deliverance*. He knew that the lock tender would not swell the boat out of the lock, especially at night, but he hoped that they would get this cargo to its destination quickly.

"What's the big hurry, boy?" a deep voice thundered.

Jonathan jumped and turned to see the lock tender looking down at him.

"I...I don't know, sir. We, I mean, the captain...."

"Oh shut up!" snarled the lock tender as he swung a backhanded slap at Jonathan.

Jonathan was too quick for him, but he dropped the signaling stone as he twisted away. Uncle James hollered to throw the line, and jump aboard. The boys traded places. Jonathan was glad to be moving again and to be away from that lock tender. He wondered if he gave away their secret when he stammered his answer to the lock tender. Jonathan reported to Uncle James what had happened, but Uncle James said that he was sure the lock tender had no idea what was going on. Relieved at hearing that, Jonathan went back to his bunk for another hour's rest.

"You'll be needed again in Syracuse," called Uncle James.

It was still dark, but the market would be full of farmers and other people who brought their goods to re-sell to the city shops. Jonathan thought about the produce that he had seen the last time they had passed the market. He wondered if sweet corn and tomatoes would be ready to sell. That always made him think of buttered corn on the cob.

"Quickly, quickly," Uncle James spoke sharply. His voice sounded anxious to Jonathan.

I must have fallen asleep, thought Jonathan.

The lights of the market were evident, as were the sounds of voices alongside the canal, some of which were languages that Jonathan could not understand. Jonathan hurried on the deck, wondering if there was trouble. Perhaps the two men on horseback had found them.

"Jonathan, lend a hand here," Uncle James was all business this morning.

"Yes, sir. What shall I do?" Jonathan asked, now that he was fully awake.

"Just keep on your toes. I mean watch out for things that don't seem right. Remember what I said before."

"Yes sir," Jonathan repeated.

"In the meantime, feed and water the mules. Be ready for your shift on the towpath."

Uncle James forced a half smile, and Jonathan thought perhaps he was a bit nervous. After finishing the stable chores, Jonathan was surprised to see that they were coming up behind several canal boats that were stopped.

"What's the delay?" he asked softly to Uncle James.

"Oh, this is the usual," Uncle James replied. "The Oswego Canal is only 38 miles long, but there are 39 locks."

"Why, that's a little more than a lock for each mile!" Jonathan exclaimed.

Uncle James nodded in agreement, and continued. "If all goes well, we could make it into Oswego early tomorrow morning. With the good Lord's help, our people should be safely in the middle of Lake Ontario, by the time those slave-hunting horsemen ride the roads of western Onondaga County and northern Cayuga County."

Jonathan was aware that he had heard his uncle speak more confidently on other topics. He decided to get ready for his turn behind the mules. He had no idea what the next hour would bring, but he thought that this next day might bring about the hardest working hours of his life.

The wait in line in Syracuse cost them several hours, but once they were on the Oswego Canal the pattern of walking, locking through, and walking again held the boys' complete attention.

Jonathan and Charles took turns walking the towpath with the mules, and then standing "guard" on the bow of the *Deliverance.* At each lock one of the two was constantly near the bell pull, ready to warn the nervous Brown family below the deck. Neither of the boys gave a thought to their aching muscles or mosquito bites. They worked all night without much sleep, and were determined to see the Browns safely to the ship that waited in Oswego harbor. Jonathan was standing lookout on the bow of the canal boat when the river next to the canal appeared to be getting wider. He expected to see the harbor town's lights soon.

Uncle James said that they would be unloading their cargo at one of the flour mills. He yelled orders to Charles and motioned for him to pull into the loading area of the large stone mill that loomed over the canal. By this time, the river, which was only a few feet from the calm canal, was racing towards the wide harbor. Jonathan could see that the Browns would have to risk going through the streets of Oswego in order to reach the ships in the harbor. Once the canal boat was secured at the mill dock, both boys joined Uncle James on the deck of the *Deliverance.*

"Boys, here's where a real adventure could start," he said softly. "Each one of us will lead two of the Browns to the schooner *Rising Star.* Jonathan, you come below, and I'll use a map to show you a quiet route to take Zeke and his momma to the harbor." He turned to Charles. "Stay up on deck and keep your eyes peeled until Jonathan and his group leaves. Then you come down and get Zack and his momma. I'll show you the route, too. Then, I'll bring the men."

Jonathan followed his uncle down to the cabin. The Browns were in the shadows at the edge of the cabin door. He studied the map, and followed his Uncle's finger as it traced the route to the *Rising Star's* berth in the harbor. He traced the route himself and stared at the pencil-drawn map until he was confident that he could find his way. He smiled at Uncle James, moved to the doorway to the deck, and turned to the Browns.

"Let's go," he said. "Time to take a few more steps to freedom."

The three walked purposefully but not so fast as to attract attention, following the route laid out by Uncle James. They saw a pair of dark figures walking toward them in the street, so they crossed over to the other side to keep their faces away from curious eyes. No one else was on the street while they made their way to the dockside.

Jonathan was relieved to see the lights of the ships tied up along the docks. The Browns pulled their hats down to cover their faces as they walked alongside the lantern-lighted ships. A sailor sat on a piling next to the gangplank of the ship named *Rising Star.* Jonathan prayed for protection, and asked the man, "Expecting any baggage for shipment to Kingston?"

"Yas, we're waitin' for six pieces," he returned.

"Well," said Jonathan with relief, "Here's the first two." He squeezed Zeke's arm, and patted his shoulder. Zeke never looked up.

His mother whispered, "Good-bye, son, thank you."

They hurried up the gangplank with the sailor, and Jonathan turned to walk back to the *Deliverance.*

Jonathan had not walked far before he was passed by Charles, Zack, and his mother walking on the other side of the street in the shadows. He was tempted to wave, but instead he looked straight ahead. In another five minutes, Uncle James came along with the men. They didn't seem to notice him as he walked by. Now that his Uncle passed by, he felt quite alone and afraid in the dark streets of Oswego. He wanted to run to the canal boat, but he was able to keep from doing so. Jonathan heard running footsteps coming up behind him. Thankfully, it was Charles catching up with him, and he excitedly began to tell Jonathan about his close call with three men who nearly bumped into them as they came around a street corner.

Jonathan tried to shush him, but Charles was so relieved to be safe, he just kept on talking. Jonathan happily saw the *Deliverance* in the distance, and the two boys finished the last 100 feet at a dead run.

CHAPTER FIFTEEN

J onathan awoke in the late afternoon to the sound of men's voices and the thudding of barrels being jostled and shoved into the boat's hold on the other side of his cabin wall. His first reaction was panic! Was Isaac's family losing their freedom?

The extreme tiredness that he felt was affecting his thinking. As he became more awake and alert he remembered what had happened only hours before. The Brown family was now safely sailing across Lake Ontario to freedom at the port town of Kingston, Ontario. He smiled to himself as he stretched his arms and sat up in the bunk. Uncle James had said that he would let the boys sleep as long as they needed before they began to travel back down the Oswego Canal with barrels of flour from one of the mills.

"Just wait 'til you see some of the paths you drove the mules on in the dark," Uncle James teased.

His voice held a tone that was full of laughter and full of pride at the same time. When Jonathan returned the remark with a puzzled look, Uncle James repeated what he had said,

"Just you wait, you'll see what I mean." Again he chuckled, "Wait 'til you see those towpaths!"

A short time later as he walked along behind the mules, Jonathan could see what Uncle James meant. The path would often cross over a stretch of water to the center of the Oswego River, where there was deeper water to float the larger canal boats. In the darkness, Jonathan had not realized that they were often walking with water on both sides—river and canal. He and Charles had been so tired that they were not aware of how different the Oswego Canal had been from the Erie.

The frequency of locking through was a break from the tedium of long stretches to walk. They enjoyed talking with other drivers as their boat went through

the locks. Jonathan was aware that it was taking longer to get to Syracuse than it had for them to reach Oswego the night before due to a line-up of boats on the canal. When it was his turn to sit at the table for the evening meal, he questioned Uncle James about the delay.

"It seems," smiled Uncle James, "that it takes awhile to get legal help to recapture ex-slaves in Onondaga County. Those two men on horseback were a mite delayed. Now they're stopping and searching all the canal boats going north at Phoenix. It also seems that we might see a little entertainment when we get down there."

"Entertainment?" Jonathan questioned.

He wondered what Uncle James meant as he hopped off the boat to begin his turn at driving. When he caught up with Charles and the mules, he repeated the story that Uncle James told him about the towpath and the river. The boys walked along together for several minutes. Then Charles turned and waited for the *Deliverance* to pull up to where he stood. He was tired and hungry after his turn at driving.

Jonathan wondered how the men could hold up so many boats and travelers without getting into trouble themselves. He got parts of the story from boatmen he passed at each set of locks.

"They're looking for plantation slaves," one young hoggee shared with him. "They busted open barrels on our boat thinkin' we had people hidden inside."

A slight shiver of apprehension passed through his shoulders and neck when he heard, "They're lookin' for a red and white boat like yours."

After he heard that, he called to Uncle James, but the wind kept his voice from being heard. He knew that there was only Oswego flour on board the *Deliverance*, but in his mind, the situation became worse than it was. He hoped that there was nothing left on board the boat that might give them away.

At the next lock, he hurried back to tell Uncle James what he had heard.

"Don't you worry, there's nothing here that would cause a problem with those bounty hunters," Uncle James assured him.

He smiled broadly to reassure Jonathan. After they locked through, they met two more boats heading north.

"How's things in Phoenix?" he asked each of the drivers.

Their answers brought back some of the anxiety of the last hour or so. He also determined that they would soon be approaching Phoenix and the two men on horseback. His eyes darted from left to right, expecting to see the bounty hunters at any moment.

As he passed another northbound boat, Jonathan saw that the captain and the off-duty driver were putting the cargo back to rights. Some of the lightweight dry goods barrels had been broken up. As he turned to watch where he was stepping, there was a shout and one man grabbed the mule's bridle as a second man with a beard grabbed Jonathan's arm and jabbed him with a thick, dirty finger.

"You!" He yelled in Jonathan's face. "Come 'ere!"

Jonathan tried to yell to Uncle James, but no sound would come from his mouth. As the rough man half dragged him toward the now slowing canal boat, Jonathan heard himself saying, "Help me Jesus! Help me Jesus!" His voice grew louder. "Help me!"

By this time Uncle James saw what was going on and was hurrying to steer the *Deliverance* against the bank.

He jumped ashore and faced the bearded man.

"Let that boy go!" he shouted. "I'm the captain of this boat. If you need to know something, you talk to me!"

Uncle James looked like he would grab the man's wrists and snap the bones. Jonathan felt the grip around him loosen, and then release. He lunged for freedom and the safety of his uncle as the man said, "We're legal slave hunters, and we're searchin' yore boat. You ain't in slave-lovin' Onondagy yet, so jest step aside." Although the man waved a drawn pistol at Uncle James, Uncle James didn't move.

Uncle James was very calm and he spoke evenly, but with power. "Man's law will someday surrender to God's law, sir, but for now you have the upper hand. Go aboard, you'll find nothing but a cargo of flour and our personal belongings."

By this time, the man who grabbed the mule had come up, and the two started to pull themselves aboard the *Deliverance*. The movement of the canal water because of the boat's momentum was now pulling the boat away from the towpath bank.

Uncle James gave Jonathan a hug, and said,

"It's all right, see to the mules—I'm going aboard to keep an eye on those men." Seeing the anxious look in Jonathan's eyes, he repeated, "It's all right. Go on."

Uncle James patted Jonathan on his shoulder. He quickly turned, grabbed the closest part of the boat's deck, and wrestled himself aboard. Jonathan thought the mules looked spooked by all the commotion, but it did not bring a smile to his face as it might on an ordinary night. Actually, the mules hadn't taken more than two steps from where Jonathan had been ambushed.

Jonathan could see lights just ahead and heard voices. Some were raised in shouts.

A man rushed up and asked, "You all right, boy?"

The man had a bulls-eye lantern that focused the light with a lens. Jonathan tried to look past the light to see the man's face. As the lantern was lowered, he could see a silver badge on the man's dark coat.

"I'm the Constable here in Phoenix," the man said.

"They've got my Uncle James!" Jonathan blurted out.

The law man brushed on past him with several other men following him.

The Constable stopped alongside the *Deliverance* and shouted, "You men! Get on out of that boat! You have no warrant to search private property!"

Meanwhile, several of the Constable's men had pulled themselves onto the deck of the boat and had disappeared below the top deck.

Jonathan was relieved to see the intruders appear on the deck with Uncle James and the other men behind them. They were soon jumping clear of the boat and hurrying down the path toward their waiting horses.

"They've busted up the cargo some, and they were just about to pull some boards out of the cabin wall before these fellows showed up," Uncle James related, "but we stopped them."

The Constable stood talking with Uncle James while Jonathan stood by the mules. Jonathan could only hear a part of the conversation,

"...law on their side, but we can't have them destroyin' cargo and mistreating honest workingmen."

He touched his cap in a farewell salute to Uncle James, and started on down the path with the other men following.

The voices of the Constable's men soon faded into the darkness. Jonathan turned to face Uncle James. The older man reached out and pulled him close in a bear hug. It helped to muffle Jonathan's sobs of relief now that it was all over.

"The Lord helped us out, no doubt about it," Uncle James whispered.

Jonathan nodded and felt the rough wool of Uncle James vest on his face.

"I know He did, I asked him to," he murmured.

CHAPTER SIXTEEN

C harles half walked and half ran up to Uncle James and Jonathan, and they included him in the big circle of hugs.

Uncle James spoke with assurance. "It's all over, they're gone, for good!" he added, the last for emphasis.

The boys smiled broadly at each other and then up at Uncle James.

"Thank you!" they shouted together, and were about to start a dance of some kind right there in the cabin, but Uncle James caught them.

"Hold on, boys, we've got a ways to go tonight." He paused, and breathed out another sentence. "No, let's stay over in Phoenix tonight. South of the locks, so we can get a good start in the morning. What do you say to that?" He held out his arms and the boys ran to him for another bear hug! Right then, no one was happier on the Oswego Canal.

The next morning Jonathan and Charles spent several hours moving broken barrels, and transferring good flour to barrels that Uncle James was repairing. They scooped up spilled flour, but had a hard time sweeping the deck because the morning dew dampened the flour and made it very sticky.

"If it rains, this deck'll look like pancake batter." Uncle James declared.

The deck and cabin were finally put back in order, and the boys sat down to a plate full of cheese, apples, fresh bread, and milk. The latter were purchased at the canal side store by Uncle James while the boys finished the cleanup. They were feeling relieved that the mystery cargo had been delivered, and that they passed through the slave hunters' trap. As soon as the light meal was over, they set about to do the chores to prepare for the final leg of the trip. Charles found himself cleaning the kitchen and cabin area and Jonathan readied the mules.

In the boys' minds, it was taking a very long time to get to Syracuse although the well-rested team wasted no time on the towpath. Locks came and went and they arrived at the Oswego and Erie connection in the early afternoon, where the barrels of flour were unloaded by several quick-moving dockworkers.

"We're picking up salt right away," Uncle James told the boys as they exchanged places from towpath to boat. "Then we'll head west. I'll need to spend some time in Weed's Basin, probably a day or two. I must take care of some personal business, see what mail has come in, and also do some banking." He took a big breath, and continued with a smile, "You hard-working boys could use some time off the canal, I'll wager." Each boy searched the other's face, slight smiles coming to their mouths. "I'll expect you both to be back before dark, though," said Uncle James. "We'll be starting out again before sunup."

The Syracuse streets along the canal and those streets perpendicular to it were filled with wagons, carts, people on foot, and people on horseback. Being a part of this hubbub was very exciting for the boys.

"This sure beats spending the summer in the shop," Jonathan said to Charles.

The *Deliverance* stopped near the Salt Works just west of Syracuse, and barrels of salt were loaded into the cargo area. The dock area was so busy that it looked like men were going in both directions at once, carrying sacks on their shoulders, and rolling barrels this way and that.

When they were on their way west again, Jonathan marveled at the increased canal traffic: packets, line boats, and many boats similar to the *Deliverance.* As the sky darkened, Jonathan noticed the heaviness of the air, and smelled the distinct odor that comes before a hard rain. Suddenly, the thunder pounded down out of the dark sky in front of him, and the mules responded with a jerk of their harness. The sound rolled along for miles. Another flash of lightning seemed to stab the earth somewhere ahead, followed instantly by more thunder. Jonathan saw the huge drops by the thousands hitting the water in the canal ahead of him. Then the mules' backs and his shirt were soaked in an instant. His face was protected a little by his broad-brimmed hat, and the rain water stained his fading denim shirt to a deep shade of blue.

The mules plodded along with their ears twitching as if in disgust over the soaking they had to endure. He looked over his shoulder for a signal to stop, but none came, and he did his best to keep the pace of the mules steady. He didn't know about the mules, but as the thunder and lightning crashed around them, he did not want to be walking alongside the canal. He wanted to get under cover as soon as he could. The rain came down even harder now.

He started talking to the mules hoping that his voice would reassure them. He nearly had to shout because of the rain and thunder, and he decided that he was not helping at all. He began to listen for the sound of the conch horn that would mean a break from the torrent of water all around him. The towpath was quickly being over-run with water. Long puddles of water were forming in the hoof print pathways of the many teams which plod in the track. It soon looked like a very long and very slender lake.

Suddenly, the mules stopped! The critters had somehow decided together that they would no longer step into the puddles. Did they think the water was too deep? Like it or not, the crew of the *Deliverance* would have to wait out the storm.

Uncle James and Charles soon appeared out of the gray mist of rain. Directions were quickly given, and soon the harness was unhitched, the gangplank was down, and the mules turned toward their stalls. Deut and Hezzy set a quick pace for Jonathan as they headed toward their dry stalls. He filled the trough with oats and hay, and he rubbed the water off their steaming backs.

After the mules were cared for, Jonathan sought the warm comfort of the cabin where the steaming stew bubbled on the stove. "This storm's going to last awhile," Uncle James predicted. "We might as well sit it out where we can be warm and dry. Speaking of dry, let's get these wet clothes changed."

It wasn't long before the boys reappeared in dry clothes, and each wrapped himself up in a wool blanket. Jonathan and Charles talked about the storm as they used thick slices of bread to mop up every bit of the savory stew.

As Uncle James came back with his own set of dry clothes on, Charles exclaimed "Great stew!"

Jonathan nodded in agreement, and added, "I'm glad we stopped."

The older man acknowledged the compliment, and said, "You boys crawl into your bunks until this storm passes by. I'll keep an eye on things so we don't block the canal the way the wind is blowing us around."

The boys cleaned up after themselves and hurried off to their bunks, wrapped in the blankets so nicely warmed by the kitchen stove.

CHAPTER SEVENTEEN

C harles was awakened by Uncle James' firm grip on his shoulder. His eyes followed his stubby forefinger as it moved quickly to Uncle James' lips, signaling "quiet." Charles slipped out of the bed covers, then followed Uncle James into the cabin where he received his instructions. "Wash up, get dressed, and get some breakfast to eat while you drive."

Charles dressed quickly while he watched the other boy, still sleeping in his bunk. He mumbled under his breath. Something about having to get up while Jonathan slept on. He chose not to remember how long he had slept in when Jonathan was out in the pouring rain a day ago.

Once in the towpath, behind the mules, his spirits improved as the sun warmed his back. He smiled to himself as he thought about the time off that Uncle James had promised the two boys for at least a part of the afternoon. He considered how he and Jonathan could be rascals on their own and still be able to stay out of trouble at the same time. Or, if they didn't stay out of trouble, perhaps Uncle James wouldn't hear about it.

"That's it!" Charles exclaimed.

The mules' ears laid back and nearly twisted around on the animal's head as if to make some sense of the outburst that came from the mouth of the driver.

Charles, now with a purpose, walked more deliberately. His head was up, his shoulders were squared, and his legs moved a little faster. The mules, however, knew nothing of the decision that had just passed through the boy's mind and were not in any hurry in spite of a little encouragement from their driver.

As the *Deliverance* passed through the village of Jordan, the cooking smells from the houses that lined the canal teased Charles' nose. Perhaps because his own breakfast was cold, hurried, and several hours ago, he was particularly bothered. He guessed it was nearer to noon than ten, and he could picture the thin slices of ham that were cooking in the galley. Charles could picture the meat slices fried so they were just crisp—his idea of perfection.

Charles had to drop the tow line several times in order to let passing boats go over their towline. He always smiled a good morning or greeted those he passed on the towpath with a "Splendid day!" As the packet boats passed, he looked for anyone he might remember from before he was rescued in Montezuma those months ago. He had listened to Uncle James reading from his Bible about keeping a forgiving spirit, but it was surely difficult to think forgiving thoughts about the boat captain who had left him for dead.

Now, footsteps sounding behind him told him that Jonathan was running down the towpath to take over for the next shift. He turned around and met Jonathan's easy smile. He wanted to voice his feelings about having to get up and work while Jonathan had slept all this time.

Before he had formulated the way to phrase his words, Jonathan exclaimed, "You're lucky!"

"Me?" Charles returned. "How so?"

"While you've been walking in the cool shade of these trees, I've been scraping loose paint from the sides of the cabin in that full sun. My arms are tired, and I'm hot and thirsty!"

Charles was at a loss for words. He was glad that he had not gotten out words of complaint about how easy his friend had it. He now stood waiting for the *Deliverance* to glide by so he could jump aboard. He watched his friend walking in and out of the shadows of the trees which were overhanging the towpath.

The gurgling of the water as it passed the canal boat's bow turned his attention to the task at hand. He got ready to jump onto the boat as Uncle James guided it close to the bank. As soon as he had clambered aboard and started for the cabin, he could see the places where Jonathan had scraped.

"Looks like Jonathan did a good job!" he called to Uncle James.

"That he did!" returned Uncle James. "After you

slice off some bread and cheese for your lunch, you can take your turn at it," he continued.

When Charles returned to the deck, he picked up the scraper, looked at it doubtfully, and made a few tentative swipes with it. Seeing how to best hold it, he started to peel the paint. After, several tries he saw that the results that he was getting were as good as the work done by Jonathan earlier in the day. He had covered several feet of the wall when Uncle James appeared to inspect his work.

"By Grannies, you know what you're doing," remarked Uncle James.

He was impressed with the way Charles was able to figure out how to use the scraper before he had a chance to explain it to him.

He thought, *This boy is a born mechanic.*

Charles soon found that some places had good sound paint and very little scraping was required. Then, he discovered that in one area many blisters appeared and as he scraped he was showered with the small white flakes. His fingers and hand were tiring from the pressure needed to move the scraper. He changed hands and soon found that he was almost as strong and skillful with his left hand as he was with his right.

He worked on in silence. The noise of the scraper against the painted cabin was the only sound he could hear on the boat. Uncle James gave no more instruction, and only the gurgle of water moving against the hull and the occasional caw, caw, caw of a passing crow interrupted the stillness of the afternoon. Time seemed to pass quickly as Charles worked on. He was intent on his task, as well as intent on impressing Uncle James with how good a worker he was.

At last, he met the place where Jonathan had started the scraping. He compared the workmanship of his friend against his own. It looked very much the same. He was not disappointed because he felt a strong bond of friendship with Jonathan. Neither one would have a need to brag here.

It was time to change both the mules and the driver. Charles was glad that he would be driving the team into Weed's Basin. He was looking forward to a time away from their chores on the canal and it was beginning to show on his face. As they approached the village, Jonathan paused from painting the boat's cabin to look at his friend's almost joyful step. He sensed that their time off might somehow get them into trouble. He had listened many times to Charles brag about escapades that he and other drivers had experienced during their time off. He knew that Uncle James would not be pleased with either of them if their behavior got them into trouble. He wondered about Charles' plan.

By the time the *Deliverance* was tied up at the dock, the crew had both teams of mules ready for the short trip to the fields of Uncle James' farm. The older man led the way to the farm, which was a mile or so west of the Basin. The boys weren't able to talk because Charles led one team down the hard-packed road with Jonathan following a safe distance behind him with the other team. The mules moved along at the same four-mile-per-hour speed that they used on the canal towpath. When they arrived at the farm, Uncle James held the farm gate open while the boys continued driving the mules right into the pasture. A couple of little yappy dogs had announced their arrival, and Smitty, the farmer walked out of a shed.

Seeing who it was he shouted, "Haloo, Jimmy!"

The two men shook hands and immediately started a conversation while the two boys removed the harnesses from the mules. The boys took turns sliding the long gate poles back into their sockets. They stood looking as the mules began grazing on the summer grasses. Jonathan broke the silence with an emphatic, "This farm is as nice as Edward's!"

Charles hesitated and answered slowly with a shrug, "Who's Edward?"

Jonathan sighed and answered, "I had a friend whose family had a farm. I used to go over and help sometimes. Before he moved."

Uncle James and the boys walked back to the canal boat and washed up. They were hungry for the thick stew that had simmered on the back of the stove all day. After they had eaten their fill, the boys shook out fresh blue shirts for their afternoon off. They stood before Uncle James, neatly dressed, faces shiny, and hair slicked back awaiting to be dismissed. With a broad smile and a warning to be good, he waved them off. They smiled at him and at each other, and quickly walked toward the buildings that lined the basin business area.

Seneca Street paralleled the canal with the building's front windows on the street, and their back windows overlooking the canal. Those that did business with both townspeople and canal people had doors on both sides of the building. A few were built of brick and were four stories tall. Some had a beam and tackle at the peak to lift barrels or sacks from the dock to the business. It was generally quieter on the street side. The canallers just seemed to make more noise.

"Where're we goin'?" asked Charles.

Jonathan answered with a shrug of his shoulders and said, "Dunno. Let's just go up one side of the street and down the other, just to see what there is to do."

"Ayeh," answered Charles.

Walking north on the left side of Seneca Street, they noticed that nearly all of the shops had something to do with the canal. At the end, a farrier had a large horseshoe for his sign. Next door a harness maker, whose sign pictured a large horse collar, and shipwright's shop sign hung from a giant boat lantern. When they reached the large general store, several children burst from the door and joined two others on the board sidewalk. Standing on the boardwalk was a pretty dark haired girl about their age. She seemed to be trying to keep the younger ones in order.

Charles eyed Jonathan, winked at him, and said to the girl, "Aft'noon, Miss."

Two of the youngsters stopped their horseplay and stared at Charles, while the others ignored him, as did the young "miss." Jonathan almost snickered at this romantic display by his friend, who now seemed stricken with embarrassment.

The uneven boards in the sidewalk tripped them up as they looked behind them for some sign that this pretty dark-haired girl had noticed them at all.

Charles, still blushing, said to his friend, "I can't believe it! She coulda said 'hello.'" He looked over his shoulder again.

After a few steps, Jonathan answered philosophically, "Wal, they don't know us."

"Don't matter," Charles blurted. "Coulda said hello."

Jonathan tried to joke about it, but a dark look from Charles ended the discussion. They walked on in silence past several more Seneca Street buildings.

Two old ladies approached, slowly and carefully picking their steps on the uneven boards.

Jonathan smiled broadly and said, "Good afternoon, ladies." They quickly returned the greeting and Jonathan gave a sideways smirk at Charles. "See, they said hello."

"Pfoof!" responded Charles, looking straight ahead.

"Don't let that black-haired girl in a blue dress mess up our day!" Jonathan said in a scolding tone. Charles kept on walking. In a few minutes, the hint of a smile touched his lips.

"Okay," he said. "Let's have an adventure."

"Like what?" Jonathan looked at him.

"Well, there's gotta be something we can do for some excitement," Charles said.

CHAPTER EIGHTEEN

Jonathan and Charles crossed the dirt street, dried by the sun and the horse and wagon traffic. A heavily-loaded freight wagon drawn by a six-horse hitch passed in front of them. Charles stood in awe of the big, muscular draft horses as they stomped their way past.

"They're beautiful," he said, but the noise of the heavy hooves, the creaking harness, and the thudding of the unsprung wagon wheels drowned out his voice. As the wagon passed, he repeated his comment. "They're beautiful."

Jonathan smiled at his friend. "Ayeh," he nodded, "they are."

Walking south on the other side of the street, the boys squinted at the sun, now lower in the southwestern sky. The breeze blew dust steadily as the horses stirred it up. The wind and dust kept them from being as interested as before in the shops and people on the sidewalk. It became noticeably cooler, and the clouds began to quickly cover the sun. By the time they crossed the bridge over the canal, still searching for their very own adventure, the west wind picked up and rain fell.

Charles raised his voice over the wind, "Let's go see the saw mill!"

They had passed a saw mill taking the mules to Smitty's pasture, and Charles excitedly told Jonathan that it would be easy to get to.

"It's not this way," he shouted to the fast-walking Charles.

Actually, Jonathan hoped that Charles was right, because he wanted to see the steam-powered sawmill as much as Charles. They both had seen several large steam engines with their wide, flat drive belts powering many shops alongside the canal.

"Maybe they'll blow the steam whistle for us," said Charles excitedly.

"Louder'n a conch horn," returned Jonathan.

They were half-way across the grown-up hay field, and the tall grass grabbed at their trousers, leaving tufts and grass seeds on their legs. They were soon at the tree line where the dark woods loomed ahead.

"You sure you know where the mill is?" questioned Jonathan.

Charles pointed confidently. "Ayeh, the road to the farm starts there at the edge of the village, and goes over there." He swept his hand in a big arc from right to left. "We'll come out on the road right near the saw mill."

The boys stepped out together toward the supposed location of the saw mill and the hissing steam engine. A breeze picked up and quickly got stronger. The wind began to whistle through the treetops overhead. High branches swayed, then whole trees began to lean to the southeast, and green leaves were stripped from the branches. Large drops splattered their faces and spotted their clothes. The rain began in earnest now, beating its way through the moving canopy of trees to drench Jonathan and Charles.

"Let's get under a tree 'til it stops!" yelled Charles.

Leaves and small broken branches blew past them. The wind was swiftly blowing from the northwest—the direction that the boys wanted to go. They protected their faces from flying branches while forcing their way into the wind, and finally reached a large tulip tree. It was thick enough for both boys to stay out of the direct wind and rain by clinging to the rough ridges in the bark.

"I never seen it blow like this!" yelled Charles.

Jonathan shook his head and yelled back. "Me neither! This is powerful windy!"

Both were seized with fear now that they realized this was not the usual summer thunderstorm. Big branches and large limbs were being wrenched from the very heart of old growth trees, thrown into other trees and onto the ground. Over the roar of the wind, they heard trees falling, pulling their roots from the earth and cracking more branches. They used both arms to shield their heads and faces from the leaf-covered branches that blew at them.

The boys cowered at the base of the tree, their rain-soaked hair whipping in the wind. They dug their fingers deeper into the ridges of the tulip's bark, because they expected to be pulled away by the wind. Parts of trees tumbled past their tulip tree and they were poked and slapped by many flying branches. First one boy and then the other cried out as he was scratched by the rough, fast moving branches. It was almost impossible to see because a massive black cloud covered them and the entire area.

They could not hear the large tulip branch above them cracking. It pivoted like a hinge and fell straight down. Jonathan turned to hear Charles scream in pain! The back of Charles's shirt was torn, and fresh blood mingled with the rain-soaked shirt. He slumped to the base of the tulip tree.

"My back!" he screamed when he could catch his breath. Jonathan gasped and wiped tears and rain from his face as he tried to see what was wrong with his friend. The great tear in the shirt allowed Jonathan to see a large ugly gash–longer than his hand, and bleeding freely.

In a glance he saw the broken branch the size of the boy's arm and perhaps ten feet long. It was a dead branch, fallen from the tulip tree which ripped into Charles' flesh. Both were near panic, Charles from the pain, and Jonathan from not knowing what to do in this emergency. As he looked around he realized that they were lost in the dark woods.

CHAPTER NINETEEN

B ack in Weed's Basin, everyone was outside looking at the damage done by the wind. In the fast-fading sunlight, they could see parts of roofs missing, and other roofs had tree branches laying on them. At one house, a large maple tree had punched a large hole into the roof and now lay in an upstairs room of the house. Pieces of glass littered the village because so many windows were blown out in the storm.

Store signs were blown off business buildings and lay in the street. Other signs lay crookedly next to a wall or a tree. The displays of baskets, tools, and clothing, had been blown off the general store front, and now lay trampled into the muddy street. In the distance to the northwest, one could see the light-colored sapwood of many broken branches contrasting with the dark wet bark of the trees.

Uncle James had already asked several men if they had seen two boys around town before the storm. They frowned and either shook their heads, or said no, they hadn't.

His concern for the boys' safety was beginning to show on his face as he continued to ask townspeople he knew if they saw the boys, "Have you seen two boys, about this high, wearing denim shirts?"

"Naw, we ain't," came the response.

Uncle James muttered to himself, "I never should have let the boys go out alone."

"Jimmy, you ever seen a storm like this?" Smitty, Uncle James' farmer friend, hollered down from his wagon seat.

His wife sat next to him, and their two small children shyly peered over the sides of the wagon box.

"No, I never, but I can't find those two boys. Nobody's seen them," answered Uncle James. The older boy whispered something to his mother, who repeated the message to Smitty.

"My youngsters seen 'em goin' through the rough piece over there." He swept his arm toward the northwest. "Hop aboard!"

The woman started to get in the back with the children, but Uncle James said, "No, ma'am, I'll ride here." He hoisted himself into the wagon box.

The horses walked down the street to the corner, and were brought to a trot by a slap of the reigns on their broad rumps. Smitty turned and spoke over the wagon noise.

"I'll fetch my terriers. We'll find 'em."

They passed the saw mill and Uncle James looked at the damage in disbelief. Many tree branches at the edge of the yard were broken, and fallen trees were lying in the sheds. Piles of lumber were strewn about the yard like match sticks. The remains of the shed with the steam engine and mill equipment were twisted on its foundation, but they saw no one.

After picking up blankets and supplies, Uncle James and Smitty used the bullseye lantern to pierce the darkness of the woods ahead. At the sound of the wagon's approach, a man with a shotgun came out of the damaged office. He stood there staring.

Uncle James shouted, "Haloo!" and kept talking as he walked closer to the man, who now raised the shotgun. "My nephew and his friend are lost in that woods yonder. I see the storm hit you pretty bad. Is anybody hurt?"

The man's shoulder's sagged and the shotgun dropped across the man's front. "My boss and a team of horses are under that pile yonder." He nodded to his right. "I shot the one horse. His back was broke, and he was screamin' somethin' awful. My boss was killed when a tree fell on the office. The other horse, too."

He looked like he was going to collapse from the shock of the calamity. The two men helped him to a bench outside the office shed. They talked for several minutes, learning more about the ferocity of the storm, the unpleasant details of the deaths there, and the damage to the property. Uncle James brought up the missing boys again.

"So, you haven't seen two boys around here, then?"

"No, sir, I ain't. Come to think of it, when I shot Buck, that's the horse, I thought I heard some yellin'. I was in a fitful state, so I didn't think nuthin' of it."

"Could we touch off your scatter gun once, and see if we hear the boys yelling?"

Uncle James wondered if the boys might be close enough to hear the gunshot.

"When I seen you comin, I figured you was gonna steal lumber, so she's all loaded up. Cap's in place."

He referred to the percussion cap that would ignite the black powder in the muzzle-loading shotgun. He pushed the gun towards Uncle James, who grabbed it, turned away from the others, cocked the hammer, and pulled the trigger. The noise echoed through the woods, and he held up his hand for silence.

The terriers cocked their heads toward the woods south of the road. One began to yip and Smitty shushed him. The men looked at each other, an unspoken question in their eyes. The man on the bench shrugged his shoulders.

Smitty whispered, "Let's loose the dogs."

Uncle James nodded in approval, and handed the shotgun back with a grim smile. "Thank you."

Smitty clapped his hands and pointed. They immediately ran off in the direction they had cocked their ears moments ago.

"Let's go!" Smitty yelled over his shoulder.

"Right behind you," returned Uncle James.

"We'll be back," he told the man on the bench, who gave a half-hearted wave of his hand.

They half ran, skipping over fallen branches

and going around fallen trees, trying to keep up with the terriers that yapped somewhere up ahead. Uncle James, although a muscular man, was not built for running through the woods, and soon fell behind. The younger Smitty easily kept up with the dogs. After ten minutes of hopping over fallen trees and twisting to avoid brush, he found the boys huddled under the big tulip tree.

Jonathan's shirt was folded into a square and placed on Charles' wounded back. Both boys were bitten by mosquitos, and Jonathan's shirtless back was covered with pink welts. Charles appeared to be asleep, and Jonathan was trying to sit up to see who was coming behind the dogs.

Smitty unknotted the sack, pulled out the blankets, shook one out and handed it to Jonathan. The other he carefully wrapped around Charles who, as he awakened, groaned softly.

"We're found, Charles," Jonathan said.

A groan was the only response. Standing now, Jonathan wrapped the blanket around himself, as Smitty looked over Charles' injury.

"You got a bad gash there, son, but it's bled and been washed by the rain, and pretty much stopped bleeding. We can put a poultice on it when we get ya ta home."

Uncle James came in, huffing and puffing hard, and seeing Jonathan, gave him the biggest bear hug of his life. There were muffled cries and prayers of thanksgiving. They went to Charles, sitting up and in much better spirits now that they had been found.

Uncle James gently put his hand on Charles' shoulder, and asked softly, "How do you feel, son?"

"My back hurts something awful, but I'll manage."

This was said with much effort to keep from crying. The terriers, sensing that all would be well, jumped and yipped until Smitty hollered and they sat still in an instant. Smitty let Charles lean on him, and using Uncle James' lantern, led the way, followed by Jonathan and Uncle James.

It took a long time to get back. They rested many times, sitting on fallen tree trunks. For a part of the way, they walked easily along a logging trail. The men watched Charles carefully for signs of weakening or fainting, but Charles was indeed strong. Uncle James remembered the story of a pale, beaten boy in the shack as told by Deacon Eaton.

Some time later they came to the clearing near the saw mill. Several lanterns flickered near the lumber piles, and shadowy figures moved in and out of the piles of boards and planks. As they came closer, they saw the dead horses, and the blanket-covered body of the mill owner. The man with the shotgun made his way over to them.

"See ya found em," he said. "It looks like you've got an injured boy there. Takin' 'im home to bed?" he asked softly.

Motioning with his hand, he continued, "We're gettin' things under control here. This sure was a killer storm."

Uncle James thanked him again for his

help, and a few closing words were said as they parted.

Smitty and Uncle James gently lifted Charles into the wagon. Jonathan climbed in behind Charles, thankful for the boost from his uncle. He sat close to Charles, trying to cushion his head from the jolting of the wagon as it rumbled toward the farm. Jonathan closed his eyes, but the sight of falling trees and an injured Charles made him open them again. Several times he was aware that the wagon stopped while the men jumped down from the wagon seat to remove tree branches from the muddy road.

The exhausted Jonathan was only slightly aware of being helped down from the wagon, and sliding between the cool sheets of the bed in the farmhouse.

CHAPTER TWENTY

C harles spent the next several days in bed at Smitty's farm, with his wife faithfully tending him using various salves from family remedies.

She came out of the room with a broad smile and announced to all, "Charles is not one to keep still for long." He walked around the house, or rather paced around the house, and finally got begrudging approval from Mrs. Smith to go outside. She saw him stretch his back and grimace in pain, but he continued to walk and regain strength.

On the tenth day, he walked from the farm to the Basin, so he could help with chores on the *Deliverance*. The walking alone was too much for him, and he had to sit down to rest for part of the afternoon.

"It's all right," Uncle James said. "You need to get your strength back first."

Jonathan nodded in agreement. After all, he had heard Uncle James say that many times in the past week. In a few more days Charles was doing some of the lighter chores, wanting to do more, of course, but Uncle James made sure that Charles did not re-injure himself. Finally, the dock-side tasks were completed, the food stocks replenished, and all three were ready to get back to work hauling goods to whatever canal town needed them.

Uncle James gave the boys the task of walking to Smitty's farm to fetch the mules, while he finalized shipment orders from an agent in Weed's Basin. He also picked up the last letters they would have until their return to the Basin. Uncle James looked with interest at the thickest of the three letters, which had been mailed in Rome. He read the penciled words on the pale yellow paper with interest, then with smiles and exclamations of "Praise God!" and "Amen!" The letter finished, he sniffed and dabbed at his eyes with his shirt sleeve. He would share this good news with Jonathan as soon as the boys came back.

As they walked from the farm with the four mules, Charles and Jonathan talked about the summer coming to a close. Jonathan said he was going back to school in the fall, because of his agreement with his father. Charles had attended school only infrequently during his difficult young life, so it mattered little to him if he went to school or not. He was ashamed that he could read and write only a very few words, even with Uncle James helping him to read from the Bible.

Once back on the *Deliverance*, they talked to Uncle James about going back to school, but Charles finally said, "I don't know what but I'll just keep on the canal, and not have to get any school-learnin."

Uncle James looked sharply at Charles, and his face softened. "Well, son, you're easily taught and I would hate for you to do less than the Good Lord intended for you to do. Some boys won't amount to much because God didn't give them the ability to think things out. They can serve in other ways, but I believe you, both of you...," He motioned with his hand. "Both of you can do much for the Lord, and for man." He leaned forward and looked across the table at Charles. "You will go to school, won't you Charles?" He paused and stared at the boy staring at him.

Charles' eyes filled with tears, he swallowed hard, and hoarsely whispered, "I don't...I...I 'spect so, sir."

Jonathan quietly added, "My father says that I should at least finish the eighth grade, so's I can read and write good, and do ciphers so I can do business."

"Well now, I think he's right, but," he poked a finger at the boys, "you're both smart enough to finish high school and be one of them fellers who figures out how to build canals, locks, and maybe even steam engines and railroads!"

Charles looked at Jonathan and his eyes brightened as he said, "What adventures we could have then!"

"Yes," said Uncle James, "if you can keep trees from falling on you." Seeing the boys' spirits drop at this comment, he relented. "Well, experience is a very good teacher, too. I didn't mean to sound cruel."

He reached into the pile of shipping orders and

receipts and pulled out his brother-in-law's letter. "Got a letter from some blacksmith in Rome," he teased.

"Uncle James!" exclaimed Jonathan. "Read it please!"

Uncle James smiled as he carefully unfolded the flimsy paper. He cleared his throat and began reading.

Dear James,

I trust this letter finds you and Jonathan well. We are the same. I have several items of good news for you to share with Jonathan. The first item is this. I was working in the shop early this month when a man walked in and introduced himself as Deacon Eaton. He told me he had business in Rome, and needed some directions. He said he would not mind being lost in town for awhile, but he said, wouldn't want to be lost forever.

Of course, I asked him what he meant by that, and he told me about how the Bible says unless we accept God's gift of eternal salvation through Jesus, we will be lost forever. James, all those years that Ellen read those words to Jonathan and me, I was blind to it. But, somehow, Deacon said that the Holy Spirit does it. Well, my eyes and ears opened to God's word. James, I understand now what you and Maude and Ellen meant. I am a believer! According to John 3:16 I am born again! Praise the Lord!

Uncle James dropped the letter, raised his hands and echoed, "Praise the Lord indeed!" He picked up the letter and continued reading.

> *The second item of good news is that Catherine has given birth to*—he paused to focus on his nephew's anxious face. *A girl! She is named Grace, and she's small but healthy. The third item concerns Jonathan. Our agreement was to allow him to work with you until the school year starts up again. That time is getting near, and I wish the boy to come home to continue his education. I came into this trade because I had to, but Jonathan should have a choice.*

The boys exchanged glances, and Charles spoke quickly. "So that's why we talked about learnin' and such."

Uncle James smiled and said, "See boys, I told you that you're smart enough to catch on quick."

Jonathan and Charles looked at each other again, and a smiling Jonathan shook his head like they both somehow were caught in a trap set by Uncle James and Ahijah Hamilton.

Uncle James said, "We'll have to sort out some details, but things have fallen into place. Don't you think so, boys? After I read that letter I went right over to the shipping agent and got a cargo for Rome. I wasn't too particular what it was because I wanted us to leave as soon as possible. So, we have a two-part load. Part goes to Syracuse, then we go on to Rome with the rest."

The boys had mixed emotions now. Jonathan was especially anxious to get home, but like Charles, he was disappointed that their summer adventure was coming to a close.

Uncle James saw this in their faces, and said, "I'd like to have you continue working on the *Deliverance*, but you'll better serve God with more schooling, like I said." Jonathan and Charles slowly nodded in agreement. Uncle James clapped his hands together and exclaimed, "Praise God in all things!" His excitement brought the smiles back to their faces.

CHAPTER TWENTY-ONE

The *Deliverance* was fully loaded with crates and barrels of late summer produce gathered from farms in the area surrounding Weed's Basin. These would be delivered to the growing market place alongside the canal in Syracuse. Then they would head back to the west end for a load of salt in barrels, through the center of Syracuse again, and they would be on their way to Rome.

During Jonathan's first shift driving east, he thought back to his trip as a passenger, remembering landmarks along the canal side that he first saw only months ago. He shook his head in disbelief as to how fast the summer had flown by! The time had been filled with chipping paint, learning how to harness, and drive the mules, and finding such a good friend in Charles.

Many west-bound canal boats passed by, and dropping the tow lines took more time than Jonathan remembered. He knew it was his impatience. He really wanted to get home to see his father, and even

Catherine, but especially his new sister Grace. Charles and Jonathan watched with greater interest the working of the locks. Charles looked at the equipment, and described in detail how the lock would operate, and he was right!

Jonathan thumped his friend on the shoulder and said, "Golly, Uncle James is right, you're a good mechanic, or an engineer like Mr. Geddes."

Charles blushed deeply and thumped Jonathan in return. "Aww, you know how it works, too!"

He was correct, but Jonathan saw the special excitement as he pointed and gestured through the explanation of the lock's operation. Charles continued his excited speech. "Say, we never did get to see the steam engine at the saw mill. I'd like to see how it works!"

"Me, too," said Jonathan. "We'll look for another one in Rome."

Uncle James blew the conch horn to remind the boys of their tasks, and soon Charles had hitched his team and stretched the tow rope after the lock opened. As they approached the village of Rome, Jonathan could not contain his excitement–his freckled and tanned face had a smile on it that he could not control.

Uncle James could see how happy Jonathan was to be close to his home once again.

You go on, Jonathan, get yourself on up there to Penny Street, so you can greet your paw and your new maw on your own. Charles and I will take care of this here cargo, and we'll come on by a little later."

Jonathan smiled at his uncle, "Thanks, Uncle

James, I'll just grab my case!" He stopped and stood in front of Uncle James. "I don't know how I can thank you for all you've taught me this summer; for taking on Charles, for showing me how a grown man of God behaves himself, and for encouraging me so much. I... I guess I'll just say thank you, Uncle James." Both man and boy stood facing one another. A deep sense of "family" engulfed them.

"Oh, go on Boy!" sputtered Uncle James. "You're going to have us both bawling like babes. Go on home!"

Jonathan grabbed his case, waved to Charles, and headed off toward Penny Street. The goldenrods swayed on long stalks by the side of the road. He hesitated before he opened the iron gate. He stood at the end of the brick walk, looking first at the house and then toward the shop. He heard the muffled sound of his father's hammer on the anvil. He put his case down on the front steps and ran toward the blacksmith shop. He stopped abruptly at the open door and stood there for a moment watching his father.

Ahijah looked up, shaded his eyes and stared at the form standing in the doorway.

"Pa, it's me," Jonathan said softly. "It's me Pa, I'm home!" he said louder this time as his father quickly set down his work and rushed to greet the boy.

The father and son stood before one another in the large open space of the shop.

"I sure am glad to see you son," he said softly. "You've grown a might taller."

Jonathan smiled in embarrassment, then he said, "I hear I've got a new sister–can we go take a look at her?"

"Sure thing, son," said Ahijah. "This work can wait. Did your Uncle James tell you more about what I wrote in that letter I sent him?" he asked.

"Yeah, he sure did," answered Jonathan. "I hear I got a 'new' Pa, too."

"I knew you were not very happy with your family when you left here last spring, Jonathan. In fact, I wondered if you'd ever come back to us," Ahijah continued. "I hope you'll forgive me for the way I'd been treating you, Jonathan. Since Deacon Eaton made it clear to us that we had to have a relationship with Jesus Christ that was personal, I'd been kind of dreading seeing you again. I know that I was a Father who was 'exasperating' my son, and I wondered if there was enough of 'the new man' in me to be able to ask your forgiveness for that."

Jonathan could hardly believe that his father understood how he had been feeling before he had left Rome the previous spring. He quickly stepped forward and hugged his father with all his might. "I love you, Pa," he said, as a lump of great proportions came to his throat.

"And you'll forgive, me, boy?" Ahijah returned.

Jonathan's head was rapidly nodding up and down. "Of course, Pa, of course I will."

Ahijah pushed Jonathan through the shop door. "Let's go and find your step-ma and that darlin' baby girl!"

The two of them quickly walked back toward the house, Jonathan stopping on the way to grab the suitcase. When they entered the kitchen, Jonathan carefully wiped his feet. In the far end of the kitchen, Catherine sat rocking the baby.

"Why Jonathan!" she cried out, "Welcome home! We have missed you so much," she said.

"Thanks, Ma," Jonathan said.

He walked across the room to the chair, squatted down by the baby girl who turned to greet him with wide blue eyes and an open mouth.

"Hello, baby Grace," Jonathan said gently. "I'm your big brother."

Glossary

Chapter 1

Ayeh - commonly used by people from New England and central New York to say yes, or yeah

Neatsfoot oil - a light oil produced from cattle hooves and bones, used to dress up and protect leather

Hoggee - a mule driver on the canal

Chapter 2

Niceties - dainty, elegant items for the house

Mercantile - a store selling many household goods

Johnnycake - similar to cornbread

Chapter 3

Wainscoted walls - the lower half of the walls in a room are covered with vertical painted boards

Challis cloth - plain, light weight cloth woven in solid colors, or floral prints

Riff-raff - disreputable people, troublemakers

Drummer - a traveling salesman

Daft - silly, simple-minded

Gi' - give

D'ja - Did you

Chapter 4

Bellows - a device made of wood and leather to pump air into the forge fire, making the fire hotter

Anvil - a large iron tool set on a block of wood, used to shape hot iron as the iron is hit with a hammer

Forge - a waist high furnace made of brick or stone used to heat iron

Apprentice - one learning a trade from an experienced craftsman

Tallow - hard greasy material from cattle, like suet

Soapstone - soft stone, smooth to the touch, makes a mark like chalk

Slag - impurities of metal, similar to a cinder

Onc't - once

Chapter 5

Gangplank - boards used to temporarily connect the boat and the shore for passengers to go on/off

Chapter 6

Lock - built with stone sides and wooden gates to raise or lower boats in the canal

Chapter 7

Lye soap - soap made from fat and wood ashes leached with water

Chapter 8

Dry dock – a channel just large enough for a canal boat. The water is drained out, providing a 'dry' place to make repairs to the boat

Chapter 10

Deacon - a layman in a church, who preaches or does the work of the church

Chapter 11

Towpath - the side of the canal from which the mules tow the canal boats

Blue Heron - a bird with long legs, neck, and bill, which feeds in the water on frogs, small fish, etc.

Conch Horn - a large sea shell with a hole drilled in the small end–used for signaling

Underground Railroad - a system of cooperation among anti-slavery people to help escaped slaves reach free Northern States or Canada

Chapter 12

Indentured - a contract which binds a person to work for another for a period of time in exchange for money or things of value

Hidey-hole - a secret compartment between walls just large enough to hide people

Chapter 13

Darkies - an offensive term to describe black people

Affika - mispronunciation of Africa

Fac' - fact

Chapter 15

Apprehension - anticipating something in a fearful or uneasy manner

Constable - a public officer who is responsible for keeping the peace in an area–not unlike a sheriff

Chapter 16

Deut and Hezzy - mule's names–short for Deuteronomy, the 3rd book of the Bible, and Hezekiah, a King mentioned in the Bible

Chapter 17

Mechanic - an artisan, a worker skilled in carpentry or machinery

Farrier - one whose main job is shoeing horses, fitting and repairing the metal shoes

Chapter 19

Scattergun - the common description of a shotgun, which scatters the B-B's as they are shot from the gun barrel

Percussion Cap - a small metal cap filled with a chemical which when hit by the gun's hammer, explodes the powder

Poultice - a soft mass of medicine which is heated and spread on a wound, then covered with a cloth

Chapter 20

Salve - a healing creamy medicine which can be applied to wounds

Ciphers - to use numbers or to do arithmetic

Bibliography

American Canal Society, *The Best from American Canals, vol 1,* 1980.
    ISBN 0-933788-32-0

Andrist and Goodrich, *The Erie Canal*, New York: American Heritage
    Publishing. 1964.

The Holy Bible, New International Version, Grand Rapids, MI: Zonder-
    van Corp. 1978.

Hullfish, Wm., *The Canaller's Songbook*, York, PA: American Canal
    Society. 1984. ISBN 0-933788-44-4

Stack and Wilson, *Always Know Your Pal: Children on the Erie Canal,*
    Syracuse, NY: Erie Canal Museum. ISBN 1-883582-00-8

Stowe, Harriet Beecher, "Little Fred, the Canal Boy" and "The Canal
    Boat" in *The Mayflower*, and *miscellaneous writings*, Phillips and
    Sampson, 1855.

Web Sites to Search

www.americancanals.org

www.canals.org

www.canalsocietynj.org

www.canals.state.ny.us

www.eriecanalmuseum.org

www.eriecanal.org

www.eriecanalvillage.net

www.historical.library.cornell.edu/cgi/bin/nys/docviewer

www.history.rochester.edu/canal/bib

www.museumlink.com

www.nationalcanalmuseum.org

www.njthc.org/booklist

www.nygeo.org

www.terrypepper.com

www.towpathadventures.com